CW00519464

"I've liked you from the get-go, Jake."

The sadness in her gaze had morphed into the sparkle he loved.

"Ditto, Millie."

"So tell me, in this situation, what would Charley do?"

His heart thumped so fast he could hardly breathe. If he went through with this and hurt her, he'd never forgive himself. But if there was a tiny chance he could make her happy and he refused to try, he'd never forgive himself, either.

"Millie, will you cancel your date with Teague and go out with me tonight?"

"To the movies with the gang?"

"No. Dinner and dancing at the Moose. Just you and me."

"I'd love to."

BIG-HEARTED COWBOY

THE BUCKSKIN BROTHERHOOD

Vicki Lewis Thompson

Ocean Dance Press

BIG-HEARTED COWBOY
© 2020 Vicki Lewis Thompson

ISBN: 978-1-946759-85-6

Ocean Dance Press LLC
PO Box 69901
Oro Valley, AZ 85737

This is a work of fiction. Any resemblance to
actual persons, living or dead, business
establishments, events, or locales is entirely
coincidental.

Cover art by The Book Brander

Visit the author's website at
VickiLewisThompson.com

Want more sexy cowboys? Check out these other titles by Vicki Lewis Thompson

The Buckskin Brotherhood
Sweet-Talking Cowboy
Big-Hearted Cowboy

The McGavin Brothers
A Cowboy's Strength
A Cowboy's Honor
A Cowboy's Return
A Cowboy's Heart
A Cowboy's Courage
A Cowboy's Christmas
A Cowboy's Kiss
A Cowboy's Luck
A Cowboy's Charm
A Cowboy's Challenge
A Cowboy's Baby
A Cowboy's Holiday
A Cowboy's Choice
A Cowboy's Worth
A Cowboy's Destiny
A Cowboy's Secret
A Cowboy's Homecoming

1

Millie Jones would be the death of him. Jake Lassiter began to sweat under his cowboy-style tux as Millie paraded down the center aisle of Apple Grove's country church in a bridesmaid dress that made him weak in the knees.

Soft material the color of lime sherbet draped her hour-glass figure and swirled around her slender ankles. It matched her eyes and looked great with her light red hair. A morning spent at Tres Beau Salon had given her an upswept arrangement of copper curls, seductive makeup and polished nails.

She was hard enough to resist in her housekeeper's outfit of jeans and a T-shirt. He'd lost count of the number of times he'd almost kissed her. Her mouth was a constant source of temptation, even when it wasn't highlighted with lipstick the color of a ripe peach.

How was he supposed to get through Matt and Lucy's wedding without doing something stupid? Well, he'd have to stay strong, even if it killed him. Before the evening was over, it just might.

Four bridesmaids to choose from, and Matt had paired him with Millie. Why not Kate Gifford, the Buckskin Ranch's new cook? Why not one of Lucy's friends from out of town? But no, Matt had become fixated on the joys of matrimony and he wanted everyone to get with the program, especially Jake and Millie. No, and hell no.

Millie joined the three ladies lined up to the left of the altar. They resembled a bouquet of wildflowers, with each woman in a different color. Clearly Lucy had chosen the colors with an artist's eye. All of the women were pretty in their dresses, but Millie stole the show, at least in his estimation.

Time to quit staring at her like a lovesick fool. Matt had decided against Stetsons for the ceremony and without a hat shadowing his face, he was liable to give too much away.

Besides, the matron of honor, Henri Fox, came next and she deserved his full attention. She'd saved his bacon as a confused teenager many years ago and had continued to be a source of comfort and support ever since. She'd done the same for the other guys gathered at the front of the church.

Warmth swelled in his chest. She looked like a million bucks. Tall, silver-haired and elegant in a lavender gown, she paused, her gaze soft as she glanced at the six men lined up next to the altar, and CJ on a stool playing his guitar for the processional.

Her boys. The Buckskin Brotherhood. A tender smile and a slight inclination of her head conveyed more than if she'd passed out hugs.

Rumor had it that she'd teared up when Lucy had asked if she'd be her matron of honor, but that sort of emotional display didn't happen often with Henri.

As she took her place beside Millie, CJ finished the processional with a flourish and played the intro to Kenny Chesney's *Me and You*. Lucy appeared with her parents on either side.

Millie had warned Jake that Lucy's dress was unique. She hadn't been kidding. The style was like many others, a fitted top and a full, floor-length skirt. But only the background was white. Swirls of color danced over the fabric repeating those the bridal party wore—lemon yellow, lime green, fuchsia, sky blue and lavender.

A crown of mixed blooms and her colorful bouquet continued the kaleidoscope effect she'd created. She looked straight at Matt and her smile reached all the way down the aisle.

"Wow."

Matt's soft murmur of awe touched Jake somewhere deep, nudging the longing he kept tucked away. He couldn't have this, didn't want it. His heart wasn't listening.

Seth Turner, the best man, said something to Matt that sounded like *hold onto this moment*.

Matt's response was clear. "Oh, yeah."

As for Jake, he'd rather not carry this image around with him for years. Too late. He couldn't un-see it. Like a penniless kid with his nose pressed against the candy-store window, he'd be tortured by Lucy's joyous expression and Matt's reverent sigh.

He was happy for Matt and Lucy, who'd loved each other since they were teenagers. Their odds of making a go of it were better than most and way better than his. Was he jealous? Hell, yes, especially when he glanced over at Millie, who had stars in her eyes.

Lucy made the trip down the aisle faster than they'd practiced it during yesterday's rehearsal. CJ adapted and picked up the tempo of Kenny's love song. Lucy arrived, a little breathless, and her parents gave her tight hugs. The ceremony began.

It was only Jake's second. He'd avoided weddings until January when Seth had married Zoe down in Eagles Nest. The Brotherhood had attended, along with Henri and Kate, but a nasty cold had kept Millie at home that weekend.

At the time, he'd missed having her there, wished he'd been able to dance with her at the reception. Life was just better when she was around. More normal.

But what used to be normal with Millie could be on the way out. A couple of days ago, Seth had arrived with Zoe and her newborn, Seth's adopted son. Millie had gone nuts over little Hamish, named after Seth's Scottish father.

During the rehearsal and the dinner that followed, Millie had held him every chance she could get. She'd looked totally natural doing it, too.

Then she'd brought that tiny bundle over to him. He'd tried cuddling the baby for her sake, but after about two seconds the kid had started squalling and he'd shoved him back into Millie's arms.

A wedding and a baby. Clearly Millie was into both. Not surprising, but if she expected him to follow her down that path, she was in for—

Rafe gave his left shoulder a slight bump. Whoops. Not a good time to be caught staring into space. He focused on the proceedings.

The words of the ceremony, some familiar from Seth's wedding and some written by Matt and Lucy, brought sighs and happy tears from the folks in the pews. Jake's gut tightened. A hell of a lot of promises in those words. A wagonload of expectations, too.

Rings were exchanged. Jake couldn't see Matt's expression, but Lucy glowed. All her attendants did, too. Especially Millie.

The pressure in his chest grew unbearable. Looking away, he drew an unsteady breath. Yeah, normal with Millie was on the way out.

Matt and Lucy kissed. It was done. CJ struck up a rousing rendition of Taylor Swift's *Love Story* as the crowd applauded, Jake included. Sporting grins a mile wide, the newlyweds hurried down the aisle. Seth offered his arm to Henri.

Jake stepped forward to meet Millie. "You look great."

"Thank you. You, too." She slipped her hand into the crook of his elbow. "It was a beautiful ceremony."

"Yes, ma'am." He shortened his stride to accommodate hers. Millie's head only came up to his shoulder, although her up-do added another inch or so. Her hand rested lightly on his coat sleeve. He shouldn't be able to feel her touch through two layers of material. But when it came to Millie, he was extra sensitive.

"Will you ever get married, Jake?"

He gulped. "I... um... don't plan on it."

"That's what I figured from the way you freaked out during the ceremony."

"I wasn't freaking out."

"Yes, you were. It was obvious."

"I had an itch in an inconvenient spot and I couldn't scratch." He braced himself for more questions.

Instead she shrugged. "Not everybody's cut out for marriage. But this weekend has reminded me how much I want a family of my own."

"I can see how it would."

"I haven't found the right guy yet." Her chin lifted. "But I will."

Her declaration sent a clear message. He wasn't the right guy, so she was through messing with him. If that concept sat like a lead weight in his gut, too bad.

2

Jake Lassiter was the most maddening person on the planet. All this time, Millie had assumed he'd avoided turning their obvious attraction into a romance because they were co-workers. But his reaction during the ceremony had opened her eyes.

He wasn't afraid of creating an awkward working relationship. That cowboy was intensely marriage-phobic. And baby-phobic, too. She'd never come across such a serious case. Not a single other member of the Brotherhood had responded that way to either little Hamish or the wedding vows.

Just her luck she preferred the one who'd panicked when she'd handed him a baby, the one who couldn't even look at her during the final moments of that touching exchange between Lucy and Matt. Damn his hide.

What had all his flirting been about? The dancing at the Choosy Moose? Oh, and the guy loved to cook! He'd handled the meals at the bunkhouse since before she'd come to work at the

Buckskin. Silly her, she'd taken that as a sign he had a domestic side.

She'd tolerated the slow progress of the relationship because the tension had been growing, especially lately. She'd been expecting him to crack any time now. Logically, it could have happened this weekend, when love was in the air.

He'd cracked, all right. She could see right through him, and he was not for her.

No point in stewing about it, though, or trying to get to the bottom of his phobia. Life was too short to try and convince a reluctant guy that having a partner and a family was a nice idea.

Time to move on. She'd fill up that aching emptiness he'd left her with. She'd find some cowboy who couldn't wait to get married. Jake wasn't the only fish in the sea, just the best-looking one she'd seen so far. She couldn't help being partial to his blue eyes and mop of wavy dark hair. Or his smile. Oh, well.

As per the usual transportation plan, she rode from the church to the Choosy Moose in Jake's truck along with Rafe Banner, the tallest of the brothers, and Kate.

"I thought it went well," Kate said after they'd all piled in and Jake had pulled away from the church.

"Couldn't ask for better," Rafe said. "Right, Jake?"

"Right."

"Not sure how you can offer an opinion, bro, since you were wool-gathering through most of it."

"Just meditating on the solemnity of the occasion. Hey, CJ sure did a terrific job. That cowboy has skills."

"He's even better than I remembered," Millie said. "Has he been practicing more?"

"He has," Rafe said. "He kicked it into high gear when Lucy and Matt asked him to play for the wedding."

"Well, it shows. Having him play was wonderful. Everything was." Except for Jake.

"I agree." Rafe loosened his string tie. "Except I'm not used to this getup."

Kate punched him lightly on the shoulder. "Don't whine. At least you get to wear pants. Millie and I are hobbled by our skirts."

"You look nice, though. Don't they look good, Jake? I'm sure you noticed that, at least."

"You bet I did. Gorgeous."

"Damn straight they are. Did you gals pick out your own dresses, or was that Lucy?"

"Lucy handled it all." Millie turned toward the back seat. "It was quite a project. She searched high and low for material that had those colors in it."

"She wanted each of us to have a shade that went with our coloring and I love this particular blue." Kate tucked her hands in the pockets of her sheepskin jacket. "But I'd forgotten how impractical dresses are, especially when it's cold out. I was glad to put this on before we left the church."

"I'm with you there. Didn't Isabel look amazing in that fuchsia dress?"

"She did. It was perfect with her dark hair."

"Isabel is Lucy's high school friend, right?" Rafe tugged off his string tie and unfastened the top two buttons of his shirt.

Kate nodded. "And Serena is her friend from college. I like them both, but especially Isabel. She's a riot."

"She is." He rolled up his tie. "Will I get in trouble if I tuck this in my pocket and forget about it?"

"Maybe," Kate said. "Aren't we supposed to do pictures at the Moose?"

"We are." Millie faced forward as Jake pulled into a parking space in front of the bar. "But if I know Matt and Lucy, the photo session will be more goofy than formal. I wouldn't worry about the tie."

"Good deal. Let's party."

"Sounds like a plan." Jake shut off the engine and unsnapped his seatbelt. "Hang on, Millie. I'll come fetch you. The footing by the curb looks dicey. Can't let you get those pretty shoes dirty."

"I appreciate it." His considerate behavior was another thing she admired about him. Why couldn't he be the man she'd thought he was? Made her heart hurt, darn it.

While Rafe helped Kate down, Jake hurried around the nose of the truck, opened her door and held out his hand. He'd done it hundreds of times. No big deal.

It was tonight. If she intended to search for Mr. Right, she'd have to break the habit of riding shotgun with Jake to the Moose on Saturday nights, or anywhere, really. She had to shake up that dynamic.

He gripped her hand a little tighter and slipped an arm around her waist to lift her over a puddle and onto the curb.

He'd done that many times before, too. Easy for a strong guy like Jake. "Thanks."

"You're welcome." He continued to hold her hand and tugged her back when she started to follow Rafe and Kate into the Moose. "Can I have a minute?"

"Okay."

"I get what you were saying back at the church."

She gazed up at him. "I hope so, because some things need to change. I can't continue riding with—"

"It's not that I don't care for you."

She could see it in his eyes. At least she hadn't been totally wrong. "I'm sure you do, in your way."

"I'm just not—"

"You've made your position clear. I'm glad the wedding brought it out. I needed to know."

"I don't want hard feelings between us."

The worried crease between his brows touched her. "You know what's funny? I thought we were getting closer. I thought eventually you'd say to hell with the risk of dating a co-worker and ask me out."

"I almost did, for Valentine's."

Her pulse sped up. "Why didn't you?"

"I knew it would turn into a mess."

"Then you've never been serious about someone?"

"No, ma'am. I always extricate myself before it gets to that point. I didn't want to end up disappointing you."

"Except you have, anyway."

"But at least it's not a mess."

"Depends on your definition."

His grip on her hand tightened. "You're upset?"

"I'm not jumping for joy, if that's what you mean. I care for you, too. I—"

"Hey, Jake, your lady's shivering." Teague Sullivan, one of the wedding guests, hopped up on the curb.

"Thanks for pointing that out," Jake said. "We're—"

"I'm fine, Teague." She gave him a smile. "We'll be in shortly."

"Okay. Don't freeze to death." He touched two fingers to the brim of his Stetson and walked toward the Moose's front entrance. When he opened the door, country music and laughter spilled out.

Jake turned back to Millie, his expression taut. "Are you saying we *do* have a mess?"

"I'm saying that many people, me included, believed we were heading in a certain direction, even if we've claimed we're only friends."

"Guess so."

"I know so." And the longer they stood in front of the Moose holding hands, the more they'd reinforce that belief. But she didn't pull away. This was the most honest talk they'd ever had and holding his hand seemed right.

She took a deep breath. "We aren't exactly a couple, but if I stop spending time with you, it'll be noticed."

"Not if we ease into it gradually. That's what I wanted to ask you before we went in—if you'll dance with me a couple of times tonight. And ride back with me."

"That's a good idea." And she wouldn't have to go off Jake cold turkey. "You need to stop flirting with me, though."

Guilt flashed in his blue eyes. "Yes, ma'am. I realize now that was a huge mistake on my part. Selfish, too. I was leading you on and I apologize."

"Why did you?"

"I like making you laugh. I like seeing your eyes sparkle. I just plain like *you*, Millie. More than I should, considering."

"I like you, too, Jake." She sighed in frustration. "But you're a royal pain in the ass."

He gave her a sad smile. "Not the first time I've heard that. Likely won't be the last. Let's go in."

<u>3</u>

That could've gone worse. But Jake wasn't happy with himself as he escorted Millie inside the Choosy Moose. He hadn't been fair with her.

Turned out they were the last members of the wedding party to arrive. In addition to his other mistakes, he was responsible for holding up the show.

A good number of the guests were here, too, and the buzz of conversation blended with the music of the country band up on the small stage. He helped Millie out of her coat and handed it to one of the servers stationed near the door, along with a generous tip.

Ben Malone and his staff had been busy today. Merlin, the large plush moose head above the bar, sported paper wedding bells hanging from his giant antlers, and wedding-themed decorations covered the rough-hewn walls.

Lucy must have had a say in the process, too, judging from the festive look of the room. Tablecloths echoed her color scheme for the ceremony, and instead of matching napkins, each table had a mixture. Small versions of Lucy's bridal bouquet sat in the middle of each table.

Millie spread her arms wide. "Look at this! Have you ever seen anything so beautiful in your life?"

"Yes, ma'am, I have."

She glanced at him over her shoulder. "Jake."

"I'm not talking about you."

"You are, too. I know that tone of voice."

"I'm thinking of the meadow trail when the flowers are in bloom." *Liar.* The meadow trail didn't compare with her.

Nothing did, especially in this moment, when the cold air had put roses in her cheeks and the breeze had plucked a few glossy tendrils from her up-do and laid them gently against the tender skin of her nape.

"There you are!" Seth spotted them and came over. "Thought we'd lost you. Almost sent out a search party, until Teague said he'd come across you holding down a section of the sidewalk outside."

"My fault." Jake cleared his throat. "I had something to discuss with Millie."

Seth grinned and raised his eyebrows. "Yeah?"

"Just something minor," Millie said. "If you two will excuse me, I see Zoe over there with baby Hamish." She hurried toward a row of tables at the front of the room.

Seth lowered his voice. "Something minor?"

"Listen, I know you and Matt think Millie and I should—"

"We do and you should. She's great and you know it. She also likes you. Everyone can see that. I don't know what you're waiting for."

"Like I told Matt, I'm not marriage material."

"Bull. You'd be—"

"I wouldn't, but this isn't the time to get into it."

"You're right. Maybe sometime tomorrow."

"I really don't—"

"We'll talk. Zoe and I are staying until Monday." He clapped him on the shoulder. "It's photo shoot time. Come on over so we can get organized."

Jake followed him through the gathering crowd. "Who's taking pictures?"

"Who else? Edna. Except I guess we're supposed to call her Ed, now."

"Ed's taking the wedding pictures?"

"You haven't noticed she's always the one with the camera when the Babes are around?"

"Not really." The Babes on Buckskins were Henri's riding buddies, all of them in their sixties except Edna, an eighty-five-year-old barrel-racing champion who'd amassed a small fortune in winnings.

They'd provided crucial support when Henri's husband Charley had died of a heart attack four years ago. They'd been a huge comfort to the Brotherhood during that awful time, too.

"Edna... I mean *Ed*... learned how to operate both still and video cameras when Hollywood crews were using her ranch and her horses on a regular basis. She loves directing traffic and she figured out the photographer gets to do that."

"I hope she doesn't have a dress code for this. Rafe's already ditched his string tie."

"She made him put it back on."

Jake chuckled. "No kidding."

"You don't say no to Edn—*Ed*." He rolled his eyes. "And Anastasia's calling herself Red, now?"

"She is."

"Can you try to keep the others from doing that?"

"How?"

"I don't know, but it's unsettling. I come back after only five months, and two of the Babes have changed their names."

"Maybe you need to show up more often, bro."

"I might have to. Millie's asked us..." Seth paused to survey the group. "Looks like Ed's started with the women. And Teague's helping her set up. We can hang out here for a bit." He turned to Jake. "Millie wants us to visit again soon, next month if possible. She's become very attached to Hamish."

"Saw that."

"It's easy to do. That little guy's something else. I didn't know babies could be so fascinating."

"Me, either." He smiled at the note of pride in Seth's voice. Fatherhood clearly thrilled him. While he raved on about Hamish, Jake kept one eye on the photography session. Teague sure was getting chummy with Millie. And Millie seemed to be lapping it up.

"The thing is," Seth said, "you won't know until you get into it how wonderful fatherhood can be."

"I'm excited for you, bro. You're obviously made for this, but to be honest, I can't ever see myself in that role."

"No? You'd be a natural."

"I seriously doubt it. Hey, this is off the subject, but what do you know about Teague Sullivan?"

Seth glanced over at the photo session. "He seems to like Millie."

"Yeah. What else?"

"Not much. Probably no more than you. Isn't he Ed's only wrangler these days?"

"He is, now that she's downsized her stable. There's a rumor going around that she's given him a house and land he'll get to keep after she's gone."

"Could be true. Sounds like her. I mean, who's she gonna leave stuff to? She has no kids, no close relatives I've heard of. Teague's been a loyal employee, seems like a nice-enough guy. Good wrangler, from what I've seen."

"In other words, he's damn near perfect."

"For what? Oh." He glanced at Jake. "If you're worrying that he'll steal Millie away, don't. You have the inside track."

"That's not the issue."

"Then what is the issue?"

"It's complicated."

"Oh, I get that. In my case, it was touch and go. Matt didn't have an easy path, either. But trust me, once you go all in, it's simple."

Jake gazed at him. "I envy you, bro. I wouldn't mind being in your position. Or Matt's."

"You're closer than you think."

"That's where you're wrong. I'm—"

"Gentlemen!" Ed's voice rang out. "I need you over here immediately!"

Seth grinned. "To be continued. Ed needs us immediately."

Joining his brothers for the photo shoot was fun. Jake mostly ignored Teague. Ed gave them stage directions with the authority of an Oscar-winner and they all whined and complained like a pack of spoiled A-list actors. Muscles were flexed and positions jockeyed for.

As they hammed it up for Ed, the rest of the Babes—Pam, Peggy, Josette and Red—joined Henri and the bridal party. The women cooked up a grading system to rate the men's performance in front of the camera.

When it was over, Rafe and Nick received top ratings for their cooperative behavior. CJ and Jake earned low marks for being goofy and disruptive. Leo was voted most photogenic, a no-brainer since he'd been teased unmercifully over the years for being too handsome for his own good. Matt and Seth were labeled classic, old-school heroes.

"Here's the secret, gents." Matt held up his left hand where a gold band glittered on his ring finger. "Snag one of these and your stock goes up, guaranteed."

"I'm all for that program," CJ said. "But my one true love hasn't shown up, yet."

Isabel waved her hand in the air. "Until she does, I'll fill in."

"That's the best offer I've had all day." CJ executed a deep bow. "I humbly accept, m'lady."

Jake glanced at Millie. She kept her mouth shut and so did he.

"Food's coming out," Matt announced. "Ed, we need to wrap this up."

"Sure thing. I just need a couple of group shots and we'll be done. Groomsmen, find your bridesmaids."

Jake didn't need to be told twice. He fetched Millie and used the excuse to wrap an arm around her waist. "I have mine."

Rafe and Kate quickly joined them. Seth led Henri over to the group as Nick matched up with Isabel and Leo fetched Serena. Lucy brought her parents over before taking her place next to Matt.

"What a good-looking bunch." Ed peered through the eyepiece of the tripod-mounted camera. "Move in closer."

Jake didn't mind that at all. With Millie tucked against his side, he glanced at Teague.

He stood in a typical cowboy pose, thumbs hooked through his belt loops. As he focused on Jake and Millie, his gaze was speculative. If he was interested in Millie and she liked him, Jake should be happy for both of them. He'd have to work on that.

4

Until tonight, Millie hadn't paid much attention to Teague Sullivan. He'd always been friendly enough whenever they'd met, either at Ed's ranch or the Buckskin. Sometimes he'd been at the Moose on a Saturday night, but he'd never asked her to dance.

He probably thought she was Jake's girl. Most folks did. During the photo shoot, she'd flirted with him a little, testing the waters. The waters were just fine. Teague had flirted back.

The evening progressed through a top-notch, Choosy Moose dinner and the cutting of a Western-themed cake. Then folks got serious about the dancing part.

She wasn't at all surprised when Teague approached the wedding party table and asked her to dance. Jake was sitting right next to her and in the middle of telling her a very funny joke. Normally she would have politely refused the invitation so Jake could finish the joke.

Instead she excused herself and allowed Teague to lead her onto the floor. Was Jake watching? She had to wait until Teague whirled her around before she could tell. Jake's gaze was glued right to them. He didn't look happy.

"I'm taking a chance, here." Teague executed a neat two-step move. "I value Jake's friendship."

"So do I." She twirled under Teague's arm. "And that's all we are to each other. Friends."

"Really?" He led her through another tricky maneuver. "That's not the word on the street."

"I know. But Jake and I aren't dating. We just... got in the habit of spending time with each other, so it looks like we're a couple, but we're not."

"Like a sister/brother thing?" He spun her around.

"I guess you could describe it that way." Wouldn't be true, but if he wanted an explanation that made sense, that was as good as any.

"I'm glad to hear it."

"You are?" The fast pace of the dance was making her breathless. That was her excuse and she was sticking to it. "Why?"

"I've wanted to date you ever since we met. But you seemed to be into Jake, so I abandoned the idea. Then during the photo shoot, you... acted different. I decided to take a chance that things had changed."

"Ever since we met? Are you serious?"

"Yes, ma'am. But like I said, Jake's a friend. And you may be like a sister to him, but he's burning a hole in me right now. Is he the overprotective type?"

"I don't know. Maybe."

"I can't be the first guy who's been interested in you."

"Of course not." She twirled under his arm again and he caught her expertly around the waist. Excellent dancer. "I've dated."

"Recently?"

"Well, now that you mention it, not for a while. I've just been... busy." Busy waiting for Jake to come around.

"Will you be busy next Saturday night?"

"Um..." Her heart beat faster. "I guess not."

"Will you go out with me? We could grab some dinner first. There's a new movie coming to—"

"I know. I want to see it."

"Great. I'll check the movie times and we can figure out the dinner plan from there. What's your cell number?"

"I'll write it down for you once I get back to the table."

"Just tell me. I'll remember."

She met his gaze. His eyes were brown, not blue. Good.

"Trust me. I'll remember."

She gave him the number and the dance ended.

"Look, I'm not going to push my luck." He glanced at Jake as he escorted her off the floor and started toward the wedding party table.

It was deserted except for Jake, who grabbed his cider and took a long, slow drink from the mug. Everyone else was out dancing, but evidently he'd decided to stay behind so he could monitor the situation.

Teague lowered his voice. "You may not know whether he's overprotective, but I can guarantee he is. Put in a good word for me, okay?"

Her jaw tightened. "Oh, believe me, I will. Thank you for the dance. I'll see you Saturday." She slipped into the chair Jake pulled out for her and turned to him. "What was that all about?"

"What?" He put on his typical *I'm innocent* expression, the same one he used when he'd been teasing her about something or other.

"You giving Teague the stink-eye."

"That wasn't the stink-eye. I was intently studying his dance moves, memorizing the steps so I could replicate them the next time I go out there."

"You are so full of it."

"I'll prove it to you. Dance with me and I'll show you I can execute the way he did."

"You don't have to prove anything. I already know you can. You pick things up very quickly. You're an amazing dancer."

"Aw, shucks, you don't have to—"

"You could have memorized his steps *and* given him the stink-eye. That would have been easy for you."

"You're making me blush."

"Jake! I'm chewing you out!"

"I know. Did he ask for a date?"

"Yes."

"Are you going?"

"Yes."

"When?"

"Saturday night."

"Where are you—"

"Stop. I'm not telling you any more details."

He shrugged. "Somebody should have the details. I mean, in case the two of you get lost in a snowstorm that night and we have no idea where to look and you both freeze to death trapped in his truck."

"You're ridiculous."

"It happens! And all because some folks don't want to give other folks details."

"I'm willing to take that risk."

"I ordered you another mug of cider, in case you were thirsty after dancing with Teague." He picked it up from Kate's place on his other side and set it in front of her.

"That's for me?"

"Yes, ma'am."

"Then why is it over there?"

"Hedging my bets. If you'd stayed out there for another three or four numbers, that cider had my name on it."

She scooted her chair around so she could see him better. "You're jealous."

"Yes, ma'am. Don't want to be, but there you have it. I've been sitting here asking myself how come ol' Teague asked you to dance and then asked you out when he's never done such a thing before."

"Because I flirted with him during the photo shoot. Figured I had to start somewhere."

"Did you have to start tonight?"

"I think so. When I was out there with him I tried to remember the last time I had a date. It's been more than two years, about when you acted like you were interested."

He met her gaze. "It wasn't an act."

"I didn't mean it like that. But you were giving off signals and I've always... you're my favorite of all the guys. You might as well know that."

"I haven't dated since then, either. Felt like I'd be cheating on you."

She heaved a sigh. "I promised myself I wouldn't ask, but I can't help it. I want to know. What turned you off the idea of marriage and kids?"

He traced a path through the condensation on the side of his mug. "I can't think of a worse time for me to go into it. No occasion is good, but..." He glanced up, his expression bleak. "A wedding reception is horrible."

"Will you tell me, though? Some other time? I think I deserve—no, that's wrong. I don't want you to tell me because I deserve to know. But if you'd be willing to share the reasons, I'd appreciate it. You don't have to, if it'll be too painful."

His expression warmed. "See, that's why I like you so much. You consider other people's feelings. If I'd stopped to think about your feelings,

I wouldn't have led you on for more than two years."

"Hey, I could have confronted you about this a long time ago. I didn't, and that's on me. But we've come to the end of that road."

He winced. "That sounds dire."

"Doesn't have to be. I plan to stick around the Buckskin and I assume you do, too. We'll be friends for a very long time."

"You won't stick around if you hook up with Teague."

"Why not? I might not live at the Buckskin, but I'll still come to work every day."

"I shouldn't tell you this, but I've heard that Ed gave him a house and some property on the ranch. He'll get that free and clear when she passes."

"So what?"

"If you want a stable situation, a husband who can give you a home and a place to raise your babies, that's a viable option right there."

"You think I'll choose Teague because he has a *house*?"

"Well, it's—"

"Jake Lassiter, I'm not the kind of woman who judges a man because he has property and money in the bank. And if you think I am, then—"

"Easy, Millie." He grasped both her hands. "I didn't mean to imply that. I know you're not materialistic. But you want certain things."

"*Love*, Jake. I want a man who loves me enough to spend a lifetime with me."

He pulled her to her feet. "Let's dance."

"It's a slow one. That's a bad idea."
"Let's dance anyway."

5

Millie was right. They were in a mess and Jake laid all the blame at his door. He'd had all the knowledge and she'd had none. At this point, he should let her go her own way and find what she needed.

But, dear God, that was hard to do! Instead of letting her go, he was out on the dance floor holding her close during a slow tune. And torturing himself with unanswered questions.

One popped out, despite his best intentions. "Did Teague ask about you and me? What the deal was?"

"He did."

She felt like heaven in his arms. Always had. "What did you say?"

"That we were just friends in the habit of hanging out together."

Yeah, like hanging out on the dance floor, her soft body nestled against his. Likely story. "What did he say?"

"He asked if it was like a brother/sister situation."

"And you said…"

"You could describe it that way."

"Damn." He stopped dancing and grabbed her hand to lead her back to the table. "I don't have a sister, but if I had one, I wouldn't be dancing with her the way I was with you." He helped her into her chair and slid into his.

"Maybe he didn't notice."

"Oh, he noticed. He landed a date with you for Saturday night. He wants all the info he can get about where he stands, where we stand. I'm guessing right about now he's confused as hell."

"He's not the only one." She took a gulp of her cider and turned to him. "Where *do* we stand? You're jealous. You want to slow-dance with me. What's going on, Jake?"

"I don't know."

"When you find out, will you tell me?"

"Absolutely. I—"

"Hey, losers!" Kate arrived and gestured toward the dance floor. "It's line dance time! Everybody's out there and I was sent to get you."

"We're on it." Jake stood and held out his hand to Millie. "Can't get into trouble with a line dance, right?"

Her smile made his heart turn over. "Not if you're standing next to me."

How could he forget? He'd been the one who'd taught her the basic line dances because she hadn't been up on them, or much of anything when it came to country living.

After she'd turned twenty-one, she'd traveled to Montana seeking something different from the Pennsylvania city where she'd grown up.

She'd had credentials, an associate's degree in the hospitality field.

But Jake had a hunch she'd been hired because she'd touched Henri's heart. Millie had been eager for a new life and Henri had always been a sucker for that. In a good way.

He stuck with Millie through the line dance, which was an easy one. Then Ed challenged them all with something tricky. Jake got Millie through it, but the gauntlet had been thrown down.

Isabel turned out to be a line-dance expert, and CJ kept up with her through an even more complicated number. Jake did, too, but Millie struggled.

He abandoned the field, along with at least half of the guests. The party was winding down, anyway. Plenty of folks were early risers.

Matt and Lucy returned to the table along with Seth and Zoe. Henri and several of the Babes were close behind.

"Everyone else can stay," Matt said, "but Lucy and I have an early flight."

Seth wrapped an arm around Zoe's shoulders. "We should take our little guy back, too."

"Hamish isn't the problem." She smiled. "He's wide awake and basking in the attention. But I'm exhausted."

"Then it's time for the grand sendoff," Henri said. "Give us five minutes. The Babes are going to handle it."

Matt glanced at her. "You have a grand sendoff plan?"

"We're the Babes."

"Oh, sorry. What was I thinking?"

"I'll pull Red and Ed from the line dance," Josette said. "We'll meet you guys in the back room."

Henri nodded. "We'll head there now." She left with Peggy and Pam.

"I'll fetch the coats." Seth left, too.

Millie looked over at Jake. "Did you know about this sendoff thing?"

"I know nothing. The way of the Babes is mysterious."

She turned to Lucy. "Were you in on it?"

"I sure wasn't. We told Henri we didn't want anyone tossing stuff at us like rice or birdseed. She promised they wouldn't make any kind of mess. Not even bubbles."

"Whatever it is," Matt said, "it involves something in the back room, and Ben's coming this way. Maybe he'll give us a hint."

The bar's owner, a fit man in his sixties, approached the group. "Everybody have a good time tonight?"

Matt offered his hand. "It's been terrific, Ben. Thank you."

"My pleasure."

"Can you give us some idea of what the Babes are up to?"

He smiled and shook his head. "Once the line dance is over, I'll make a short announcement that you and Lucy are taking off so everyone can gather near the door. Then the band will start playing your getaway music."

"But we didn't choose—"

"The Babes picked something. They'll come out and take their positions."

"Positions?" Lucy's eyebrows lifted.

"Don't worry. It'll be obvious what you're supposed to do." The line dance ended. "That's my cue. Have fun." He walked up to the mic and made his announcement.

When the band launched into Tim McGraw's *I Like It, I Love It*, the Babes danced out of the back room. They each held a pole aloft that they'd wound with sparkling fairy lights and silk flowers in Lucy's color scheme.

"Oh, my goodness." Lucy's hand went to her mouth.

Matt shook his head. "That's pretty, but I don't—"

"They're going to create an arch for us to pass under. I love them so much." She turned to Matt. "I love you so much."

Millie's vision blurred. Such a happy couple. She would have a love like that. Someday.

<u>6</u>

Matt and Lucy took off, dashing under the crossed sparkling flower-covered poles while the guests clapped and cheered. It was done. Another member of the Brotherhood was married. Eventually the others would do the same, leaving Jake as the lone wolf. As Josette would say, *c'est la vie.*

He returned to the table with the rest of the wedding party. Although the band was still playing, nobody in their group seemed inclined to dance. Seth and Zoe were packing up, so Millie offered to hold the baby while Zoe spread a blanket in the carrier.

When the little guy's admirers clustered around Millie, Seth grabbed the opportunity to take Jake aside. "I really would like a chance to talk tomorrow," he said in a quiet voice.

"I have barn duty in the morning."

"I'll be there." He glanced at Millie. "She's a gem."

"Yep. But I—"

"We'll talk in the morning." He gave Jake's shoulder a squeeze and walked over to Millie.

"Hate to deprive you of that kid, but we're taking him home with us."

"Can't," Millie said. "He's grabbed hold of my finger and won't let go. You'll need the Jaws of Life to pry him loose."

"I read about that," Kate said. "Newborns have a strong grip. Supposedly if you lifted your hand, he could support himself just by hanging onto your finger."

"Is that so?" CJ, his blond hair darkened with sweat from dancing, moved in closer and peered at the tiny fist. "Let's try it."

"Let's not." Seth lifted the baby from Millie's arms, leaned down and kissed his pink cheek. "Turn her loose, Hamish. You're going home with your mom and me."

The baby yawned and let go of Millie's finger.

"Good job. Thanks, buddy." Seth deposited him on the blanket Zoe had arranged in the carrier.

"No way he let go on purpose," CJ said. "You were just lucky."

"It's not luck." Seth wrapped the blanket around Hamish and tucked it in. "He responded to my tone of voice and relaxed his grip."

"If you say so. I don't know much about these little dudes. I'd sure love to see that dangling trick, though. We wouldn't let him fall."

Seth flashed him a smile. "You need to get your own baby, bro."

"First I need a lady who'll have me."

"You'll find her." Seth picked up the baby carrier. "See you folks tomorrow."

Zoe buttoned her coat. "Catch you all later!" She walked away with Seth.

"Poor CJ." Isabel looped an arm around his shoulders. "Can't find the right woman. Maybe you should move to Seattle."

Rafe chuckled. "Good luck turning that cowboy into a city slicker."

"Rafe's right." CJ slipped an arm around her waist. "I'd wither up and die in the city. Any of us would."

"I can't imagine living where there's a bunch of traffic," Nick said. "Even Great Falls has too much for my comfort."

Leo nodded. "I was thinking that last week when I had to pick up a part for my truck. Couldn't wait to get back here."

"Try living in a city with millions of people." Serena made a face. "And almost all of them drive."

"Not for me." Millie shuddered. "I used to be okay with city driving, but now I don't like it at all. Apple Grove's roads suit me perfectly."

"It's a nice little town," Isabel said, "but you only have one movie theater. That's crazy."

"But it's a great old theater," Jake said. "Beautiful woodwork and antique light fixtures, and they've kept it up. Which reminds me, I haven't seen the movie that just started last week, the one about the dog and the little girl."

"I want to see that." CJ turned to Isabel. "Want to go tomorrow night?"

"I've seen it. I mean, I could see it again, just to go with you guys. It's worth a second look."

Serena nodded. "I went weeks ago. But it's good, so if everybody's going, I will, too."

"I'm in," Leo said.

Kate, Rafe and Nick all agreed to go. But Millie stayed silent, even though Jake knew she loved feel-good movies like this.

He turned to her. "Are you in?"

"No, thanks." She avoided his gaze.

"But isn't this the one you told me about, the one you especially wanted to see?"

"Yes, and I'll be going next weekend."

"Oh." The light dawned. "You could see it twice."

"That seems like... preempting."

"No, it's not. It's going once with your friends and then later with your... date." He almost choked on the word.

"Millie has a date?" CJ stared at her. "Who with?"

Kate gave him a look. "That's her business."

"Do you know?"

"No, I don't, and I'm not going to ask."

"The heck you won't," Nick said. "You're roommates. You tell each other everything."

"This just happened." Millie glanced around the group. "And it's no big deal. Teague asked me to dinner and a movie, that's all."

"Now that you mention it," Rafe said, "I saw you dancing with him."

CJ frowned. "He's a nice guy and all, but I don't see you two together."

Millie blew out a breath. "It's only a date, CJ. One date doesn't mean we're *together*."

"That's good, because he's not—"

"CJ." Jake glared at him although he was secretly happy that CJ was running interference. "Kate's right. It's not our business."

"In a way, it is," Nick said. "I mean, if we thought Millie was going out with a dirtbag, wouldn't we try to stop her?"

"But Teague's not a dirtbag," Rafe said. "Ed wouldn't hire a sleazy cowboy. I've heard that she gave him a little house and a plot of land."

"I heard that, too." Leo glanced at her. "You must like him or you wouldn't be going on this date."

"I like him." Millie looked at everyone but Jake. "And I don't feel right going to the movie tomorrow night when I'll be seeing it next Saturday night with him. That's the long and short of it. Can we move on?"

Jake sighed. "Please, let's move on."

Nick consulted his phone. "There's a seven o'clock showing. We'll need to organize transportation. Since Millie's not going, there's space in Jake's truck and we can take mine, too."

Once Nick announced there was space in Jake's truck because Millie wasn't going, the conversation became an annoying buzz. Jake didn't care who rode with him. If that person wasn't Millie, their identity didn't matter.

The number of guests dwindled quickly in the next half-hour. When the Babes said their goodbyes, the Brotherhood concluded it was time to leave, as well.

Millie rode shotgun on the way home, as usual. But the flirtatious mood they'd enjoyed for the past couple of years had evaporated. Rafe and Kate didn't have much to say, either. Maybe they were tired, but maybe they'd picked up on the change in Jake and Millie's relationship.

When they arrived at Kate and Millie's homey three-bedroom cottage, Rafe climbed out to see them to the door while Jake kept the motor running. In the past, the ladies had often invited them in for a nightcap. Not tonight.

Rafe returned and swung up into the seat Millie had just vacated. He closed the door and buckled up. "Okay, Jake, what the hell is going on?"

Jake put the truck in gear and pulled away from the cottage. "After the ceremony, as we were heading down the aisle of the church, Millie asked if I ever planned to get married."

"Pointed question, considering."

"Fair question. I've been stringing her along, Rafe. In my heart, I knew she wanted to settle down one day with a husband and kids. I *knew* that, and yet I continued to flirt with her, dance with her, pretend it was going somewhere because…"

"Because?"

"Being with Millie is the sunshine in my days, the starlight in my nights. But it's not fair to monopolize her time and keep her from connecting with other guys. I can never give her what she wants. I'm a selfish bastard and she'd be well rid of me."

"Whoa."

"I should be horse-whipped. Do they do that anymore?"

"I don't know. I was never clear on what that meant, but you won't find anybody around here willing to do it. I take it you're anti-marriage?"

"Not for other people. Seth and Zoe seem to be in good shape. Matt and Lucy probably are, too."

"What's this *seem to be* and *probably* stuff? Those two couples are solid."

Jake sighed. "I'm sure they are. I don't trust myself in this area, so it's hard for me to look at happy couples and be convinced they'll stay that way. Seth is coming down to the barn in the morning to work on my mental attitude."

"Good. I had no idea you were so screwed up."

He laughed. "Really? I thought it was obvious."

"About this, I mean. We're all screwed up in one way or another or we wouldn't be here. You're so good with the ladies that I never guessed you were paranoid about getting hitched."

"It's my dirty little secret."

"But now it's out."

"To Millie, at least, and that's why she accepted the date with Teague. I'm not right for her and she needs to find someone who is."

"How do you feel about that?"

"I'm chewing nails."

"Gonna let her go out with that guy?"

"If that's what she wants, she should go on that date. He might be exactly right for her."

"He's not, and you know it. You're right for her. You always have been. Everybody sees that."

"I'm not right. I'm too messed up."

"Then we need to fix you. Matt's leaving, but at least Seth is here for another day, so we're nearly at full power."

Jake pulled up next to the bunkhouse and shut off the motor. "You guys can't fix me."

"Sure we can. We're the Brotherhood."

7

Kate closed and locked the door of the cottage. "Look, I don't want to get all up in your business, but—"

"Oh, please do." Millie took off her jacket and hung it in the front hall closet. "I need to talk this out with somebody besides Jake."

"Care for a spot of tea?"

Millie laughed. "And crumpets. Do we perchance have crumpets?" Her roommate had a treasured set of teacups and a teapot her English grandmother had willed to her. Using them seemed to require speaking like Brits.

Kate hung up her jacket. "We're fresh out of crumpets, but we have brownies. Let's take off these dresses and get into our jammies. Then we'll talk."

"Great plan." She headed into her bedroom to change.

Kate beat her to the kitchen and already had a plate of brownies on the table and tea brewing. Until Kate had arrived with the loose-leaf kind, Millie hadn't liked tea. Now she was a fan.

Kate poured tea into both cups and added honey to hers. "I'm guessing the Teague deal has something to do with the conversation you had with Jake in front of the Moose tonight. Did he tick you off?"

"Kind of. Except I'm not mad at him anymore."

"You aren't? Then why did you give him the silent treatment on the way home?"

"The way we used to act with each other won't work for me anymore." She stirred honey into her tea. "I'm tired of the surface relationship we've had going on. Matt and Lucy's wedding was a wakeup call." She glanced over at Kate. "I want to get married."

"Hm." Kate picked up a brownie and took a bite.

"You're thinking I have wedding fever."

She chewed and swallowed. "It's been known to happen. Add in Seth and Zoe's baby boy, and even I was rethinking my choices."

"That's just it. I haven't made a choice. I'm drifting. I've always assumed I'd get married someday, but I figured I had plenty of time."

"You do. Don't rush it. I got married because I was following some imaginary timetable. Worst decision of my life."

"How old were you?"

"Twenty-two."

"Well, I'm twenty-eight. Zoe's around my age. Lucy's a couple of years younger. Time's passing for me and I—"

"Hold your horses, kiddo. First you'd better make damn sure you've found Mr. Right. If you marry Mr. Barely Adequate because the clock is ticking, I promise you'll live to regret it."

"Yeah, well, don't laugh, but I thought Jake was Mr. Right."

"Jake? Have you even kissed him?"

"No. But I'm attracted to him and we have fun together. Lately he's been giving me The Look." She picked up a brownie.

"The one that sets your panties on fire?"

"Yep." She bit into it. Delicious.

"How did I miss that?"

"He doesn't do it often. We're always in a crowd and he probably wouldn't want to be caught giving me lustful glances. Come to think of it, I don't think we've ever been truly alone. But I can tell he wants me. And I want him, too." She took another bite of her brownie. It didn't substitute for what she craved, but she couldn't have that so she'd take a brownie, instead.

"That's a good beginning." Kate sipped her tea. "But clearly something happened to derail things between you two."

"Turns out he has no interest in marriage."

"Ah. I can't say I'm surprised, but why not?"

"I don't know, and we had no chance to talk about it."

"Aren't you curious?"

"Sure, but I won't try to talk him into the idea."

"God, no. Any guy who needs to be talked into marriage is the opposite of Mr. Right." She took another brownie. "I sort of agree with CJ about Teague, though. He doesn't seem like your type."

"Why not?"

"Too serious. One of the things I love about Jake is that he laughs a lot. I'm trying to remember if I've heard Teague laugh. I have no memory of it."

"He probably does. You spend way more time around Jake. We only see Teague when we go over to Ed's with the Babes for their barrel racing practice."

"I suppose. Personally, though, I couldn't spend my life with a man who doesn't have a working funny bone. I don't care how gorgeous he is."

"I'll be spending an entire evening with Teague next Saturday. I'll bet he'll laugh sometime during the night. For one thing, he won't be getting the stink-eye from Jake."

Kate's eyebrows lifted. "Jake did that tonight?"

"Oh, yeah. He glared at us the whole time we were dancing."

"He's jealous?"

"He admitted it. But I can't worry about that. I'm moving on."

"What about that pesky issue of wanting to get naked with him? I doubt that urge will disappear overnight."

"You know what? It's only a fantasy. Like you pointed out, I haven't even kissed that cowboy. He might be a lousy kisser and a terrible lover. Hey, maybe that's why he doesn't want to get married. He has performance anxiety."

Kate grinned. "Keep telling yourself that, girlfriend."

* * *

With more guests in the cabins due to the wedding, Millie had a heavier work load than usual the next morning. Fine with her. The busier she kept herself, the less time she had to focus on Jake.

She saved Zoe and Seth's cabin for last and texted Zoe to see if Hamish was asleep. She could always come back later.

Come on over, Zoe texted back. *I'm giving Hamish his bath. Seth's down at the barn.*

Perfect. She could spend a little time with them before taking a cart of linens to the laundry room.

She knocked and opened the door a crack. "It's Millie."

"Come on in. I could use a hand with this slippery little guy. I'm not used to the bath routine yet."

Leaving her cleaning supplies outside on the porch, she stepped into the cabin and closed the door. "I'm no expert, either." She walked toward the bathroom. "I helped with my niece when she was about this age, but I—good grief."

"I know." Zoe glanced up from the bathroom sink while keeping a grip on the wiggling baby. "We've splashed water everywhere. The towels I planned to dry him with are soaked. Sorry. You don't have to deal with it. I'll—"

"No worries." She glanced at Hamish. "I think he likes it."

"Oh, he *loves* it. This is only his second bath, since I had to wait until his umbilical cord healed, and he gets so excited when I lower him into the warm water. Then he pees, and that's a whole other issue."

Millie swallowed her laughter. "I'll get you some dry towels from my cart."

"Thanks. I thought Seth would be back by now. He wanted to go down and help Jake and Rafe feed, but shouldn't they be done?"

"Usually. Be right back." She went out to her cart, grabbed a stack of clean towels and hurried to Zoe's and Hamish's rescue. She held out a towel. "Let's wrap him in this. Then I can take him into the living room while you get out of those wet clothes."

"You're a lifesaver." She nestled the dripping baby in the folds of the towel.

Millie folded the towel around his precious little body and carried him out of the bathroom. He was good as gold, staring up at her with eyes that could go blue or brown. Too early to tell. But he was studying her, no question.

If she and Jake had a baby, the kid could end up with green like hers or blue like Jake's.

Jake's baby. That had been part of her fantasy, too. He would be a wonderful lover, husband and father. His sense of fun would make every day an adventure.

Oh, yeah, she'd invested heavily in that dream. She'd based it on such shaky evidence, too—some flirting, some hot glances, and Jake's love of cooking. She should have known better. Kate loved to cook and she was death on marriage.

Zoe came out of the bedroom in dry clothes. "I should have waited for Seth. But I ran out of things to do and Hamish was awake, so I decided to tackle it on my own."

"No harm done. It's only water."

Zoe grinned. "And some pee."

"Hey, it's what babies do. Although with my niece it was easier. More contained."

"I know! I'm never prepared for the fountain to erupt." She held out her arms. "I'll take him, now. I'll get some clothes on him so he's ready to go out into the world when Seth gets back."

"I'll grab my cart and start on the bathroom, if that's okay."

"That would be great. I'm so glad I got to meet you at last. I hated that you had to miss Seth's and my wedding."

"I hated it, too, but trust me, you wouldn't have wanted my germs down there." Would Seth's wedding have affected her the same as Matt's?

Maybe. It wasn't only the timetable, as Kate had implied. It was also the joy that each of these couples had found by joining forces against whatever Fate dished out.

She had friends—good, solid folks who would always support her. She had family—her parents, her brother and his wife and kids. But she wanted a partner who was always there, who stood by her side through thick and thin.

As she was mopping up the bathroom, her phone pinged. Could be anybody. But it wasn't. It was Jake.

Can we talk? I'd like some privacy. Maybe in your cottage around noon? Kate should be involved in the lunch routine at the dining hall. I can bring some food to share. Let me know.

Sounded innocent enough, except that they'd never had a truly private moment alone. Heart thudding, she texted back. *Sure, why not? Bring whatever you feel like eating. I'm not picky.*

Not about food, anyway. She was picky about men. And damn it all, Jake was still her first choice.

_8_

Jake was sweating bullets as he pulled up in front of the white clapboard cottage that Millie shared with Kate. He knew the place well since Seth's mom had lived here. Seth had, too, until he'd turned sixteen and requested a transfer to the bunkhouse.

Jake had arrived at the Buckskin a couple of years after that. He and Matt had been the new guys, both wondering if they'd fit in. Having Seth around, a wrangler their age, had helped.

After shutting off the engine, Jake picked up the bag of sandwiches and climbed out. His breathing was still wonky, so he took his time going up to the porch.

The weathered Adirondacks were the same ones he'd sat in during summer evenings with Matt, Seth and his mom. She'd bring out big bowls of popcorn and a pitcher of homemade lemonade. Once they were of age, it had often been bottles of hard cider instead.

He could use some of that Dutch courage about now, but it was too early in the day. And too cool to sit on the porch. He dragged in a breath.

Either he took this road or he'd have to step back and let Teague make his move. He rapped on the screen.

Millie opened the door immediately. She looked as nervous as he was. And beautiful. She always wore her hair in a ponytail for work, but now it fell to her shoulders in waves of burnished copper. For him?

She didn't smile. "Come in. I have coffee."

"Great." He held up the paper bag as he walked through the doorway. "I made us a couple of sandwiches." Fixing them was one thing. The knot in his stomach might interfere with eating them.

"I set us up in the kitchen."

"Sounds good." Damn, he still couldn't seem to breathe normally. Carrying the sandwiches into the kitchen, he put the bag on the table. She'd set their places, the ones they always took when the four of them hung out here.

Except today, for the first time ever, it was only them. Two empty chairs underscored the situation. Noon light coming through the kitchen window made everything look different, too.

He laid his hat brim-side up next to his place. One night he and Rafe had taught Kate and Millie how to flip cards into an upended hat. Those women must have practiced like crazy after that, because now they were unbeatable.

He took off his jacket and draped it over the back of the chair he usually sat in.

"Here's your coffee." She brought over two steaming mugs and put one by his place and the other by hers.

"Thanks." He helped her into her chair before sitting down, himself. Opening the bag, he pulled out the wrapped sandwiches and handed her one. "This all feels very weird."

"Yep." She unwrapped her sandwich and laid it on her plate. "Oh, I forgot. There are chips in the cupboard if you want me to get—"

"I don't need 'em. I'll be lucky to get through this sandwich."

"Then why did you bring food?"

Surprised by the question, he glanced at her. "It's our lunch hour. We both need to eat."

For the first time, she smiled. "That's so you. You never want anyone to miss a meal."

"It's not good to skip meals. It messes with your digestion."

"So you're going to force down this sandwich, even though you're so uptight that you don't want it? That can't be good for your digestion, either."

He gazed at his sandwich. "You have a point."

"What if we wrap up the sandwiches and stick them in the fridge until after this talk that has you tied in knots?"

"Okay." He rewrapped the sandwich and put it in the bag.

She did the same and got up. "Do you still want your coffee? I could put that in a thermos."

"I'd like to keep the coffee. Gives me something to hold onto." When she returned to the table, he stood and helped her into her chair again.

Then he reclaimed his seat and wrapped his hands around his coffee mug. Good thing it was a generous size and not one of the little teacups the ladies were so fond of. In his current condition, he might crush that delicate china.

Millie took a sip from her mug and put it back on the table. "Well?"

"The guys think—" He stopped to clear his throat. "They think I need to tell you why I don't plan to get married. At the bare minimum, you deserve to know that."

"Did you have a meeting of the Brotherhood?"

"Not exactly. Well, sort of. Rafe and I talked on the way back to the bunkhouse last night. Then we discussed the situation with Leo, Nick and CJ. We decided not to text Matt."

"I should hope so."

"We didn't bother Seth, either, but I knew he was coming down to the barn this morning, so he'd have a chance to put in his two cents."

"Do they know the reason why you don't plan to marry?"

"They do now."

"They didn't know before?"

"It never came up."

"How could it not come up? You live together, work together, party together. Oh, wait. Never mind. I get it."

"Get what?"

"Guys. Everything is on a need-to-know basis."

"Right. And now you need to know, so here I am."

That seemed to amuse her and she ducked her head, but when she glanced up, her expression was serious. "Thank you for that. I'm all ears."

He gathered his forces. Seth had assured him that talking about his miserable past would get easier. So far it still sucked. "My parents have been married four times."

Her eyes widened. "That's a lot."

"To each other."

"What?"

"They've married each other four times over the past thirty-some years."

"Then they've divorced three times?"

"Four. They're currently divorced. I found that out when I talked to my dad this past Christmas. But he's sure they'll get back together. With their history, they probably will."

"That's... that's... I don't—"

"Don't know what to say? Whether to laugh or not?"

"There's nothing funny about it. Do you have any brothers or sisters?"

"Not that I know of. My mom's convinced my dad fathered some kids when they were divorced, but he claims he hasn't. They fight about that a lot, but they can get into a screaming match about little stuff, too. Like how to hang the toilet paper roll."

Millie shuddered. "Your life must have been chaos."

"I spent most of my time with friends or locked in my room. They hardly seemed to notice."

"And I'm guessing meals were haphazard."

He nodded. "I tried putting myself in charge of the kitchen, but any meal I cooked had the potential to end up with dishes hitting the wall, so I gave up on it."

"My God."

"The divorces brought the most drama, but in between divorces they'd have trial separations. They were cheaper and kept the pot well-stirred. I think the record was four of those between my seventh-grade year and graduation from high school."

"Zero stability."

"You've got it. It was more peaceful when my dad was gone, although I didn't see much of my mom. She'd be busy dating. They both dated. Then my dad would come around with a dozen red roses and it would start all over again. I don't much like red roses."

"I promise not to give you any."

He met her gaze, thinking she was making a joke. Instead her soft green eyes looked so sad, sadder than he'd ever seen them. "I'm depressing you. I'm sorry. That's the gist of it. We can change the subject."

She reached over and squeezed his arm. "I'm not depressed. I'm horrified on your behalf. No wonder weddings freak you out." She didn't move her hand.

Her warmth penetrated through his sleeve. Nice. "Fortunately I've managed to avoid going to them. Seth and Zoe's was the first. It wasn't too bad, maybe because it wasn't in Apple Grove. I don't know Zoe that well. But Matt and Lucy, that's close to home. If they turn out like my parents..."

"They won't." She gave his arm another squeeze.

"I hope not." He took a shaky breath. "But I might."

"Do you really think so? Wouldn't you do everything in your power *not* to be like them?"

"Oh, I'd try, but I've read the research. Kids who go through stuff like that learn the pattern. I'm a bad risk, Millie."

She tightened her grip on his arm. "What if I'm willing to take it?"

He swallowed. Seth had predicted she'd react this way. His heart beat faster. "I could be putting you in harm's way. Teague's a solid guy. I seriously doubt he has scary demons. You would—"

"But I don't want Teague."

"You must want him a little bit. You accepted a date with him."

"Only because I thought you were a hopeless case."

"I probably am." But he didn't move his arm and she didn't take her hand away.

"Is that what the Brotherhood thinks?"

"Well, no, but they're gonna be in my corner, no matter what. We have our oath. We have our creed."

"What would Charley do."

"Yes, ma'am. If I thought I could be half the man Charley Fox was, I'd tell you to cancel that date with Teague and go out with me."

"Let's think about that creed. When Charley met Henri, he'd been through a divorce, right?"

"Yes, but—"

"He must have had some self-doubt about whether he'd make Henri a good husband since he'd already had a breakup."

"It's possible."

"What if some guy who hadn't been divorced had wanted to date Henri? Would Charley have stepped aside to make way for a better prospect?"

"If he had, Henri would have been very unhappy with him. She's told me how much she liked him from the get-go."

"I've liked you from the get-go, Jake." The sadness in her gaze had morphed into the sparkle he loved.

"Ditto, Millie."

"So tell me, in this situation, what would Charley do?"

His heart thumped so fast he could hardly breathe. If he went through with this and hurt her, he'd never forgive himself. But if there was a tiny chance he could make her happy and he refused to try, he'd never forgive himself, either.

"Millie, will you cancel your date with Teague and go out with me tonight?"

"To the movies with the gang?"

"No. Dinner and dancing at the Moose. Just you and me."

"I'd love to."

9

"Wow, that's messed up." Kate sat on the living room sofa with her feet on the coffee table. She'd joined Millie for their usual afternoon cup of tea before she left for the dining hall to start dinner for the guests. "I can understand why he's steered clear of wedding bells. Parents like that can scar you for life."

"But maybe he can heal." Millie had pulled the rocker up to the coffee table so she could prop her feet on the other side of it.

"Maybe. But I thought you weren't into convincing a reluctant man."

"I'm not. The minute he starts backing away, I'll let him go."

"Even if you're up to your eyeballs in love with him?"

Millie hesitated.

"Aha! You're half in love with him already."

"How can I be? I haven't kissed him yet!"

"I haven't kissed Captain America, either, but I'm totally in love with him."

"Captain America is a fantasy."

"Much as I like Jake, he is, too. Yesterday he was the one you couldn't have, which puts him in Captain America territory. Today he's a wounded hero, and don't we all go for that? Our love will heal his tortured soul and make him whole again."

"You're jaded."

"I'm realistic. And I speak from personal experience. Please learn from my mistakes."

"I'll keep your advice in mind, but I'm going on this dinner date. And I'm determined to kiss him before the night's over."

"Just kiss?"

"Absolutely! Jumping into bed would be a huge mistake. Not to mention that I'm sharing this place with you and he lives in the bunkhouse."

"There's always the backseat of his truck."

"Blech. If I ever get naked with him, it won't be in the backseat of his truck."

"I'm open-minded. If you want to bring him here, I'll wear earplugs."

"Kate, stop it! Jake and I are not having sex tonight. We're miles away from that step." She blamed the tea for her slight flush.

"I estimate you're about a block away from that step. You two have been building up a head of steam ever since I came to work here. Once you kiss him, or he kisses you, whichever happens, it'll be all over."

"Nope. We'll take it slow. I mean, we were alone for at least an hour while we talked and then ate our sandwiches. He didn't try to kiss me, or even hug me when he left."

"I have a theory about that. He didn't want to start something he wasn't prepared to finish. He wouldn't have come over here with a condom in his pocket. That's not Jake."

"It sure isn't!" She put down her teacup and stood. "It's too hot in here. I'll bet the thermostat's—"

"There's nothing wrong with the thermostat." Kate grinned. "It's you, toots."

She sighed. "Okay, so I'm excited about the prospect, but we're not rushing into anything."

"I don't see why not. Unless you've been sneaking out, you haven't dated anyone since I came on board."

"I'm not the sneaking out type. I would have told you if I'd gone out with someone."

"I figured that. I don't recall Jake having some sweetie in the time I've been employed, either."

"He hasn't. He said it would have felt like he was cheating on me if he got involved with someone else."

"I rest my case. You're a couple of powder kegs ready to blow."

"You're wrong. We're both capable of restraint."

"I'll wear my earplugs to bed tonight, just in case."

Pulling the lumbar pillow from behind her back, Millie threw it at her.

Kate ducked and the pillow sailed over her head and onto the floor. "You'll see. I'm older and wiser. Just be careful."

"Don't worry. We won't be doing anything tonight, but even if we did, I'm a fanatic about birth control."

"Not my concern. I'm worried about your heart."

"It's been broken before."

"I'm sure. By some boy with no sense. But Jake's a grown man with enough charm and charisma to light up the town of Apple Grove. If he breaks your heart, it's gonna leave a mark."

* * *

Millie put extra time into getting ready for her date. Her efforts didn't compare to Saturday's makeover for the wedding, though. She'd never looked that good in her life, but the elaborate hairstyle and fancy dress didn't represent the real Millie Jones.

A pair of tight, stylish jeans, her favorite boots and a knit top in forest green was more like it. She left her hair down and tamed the natural curl with a brush and blow dryer.

She glanced at the clock. Five minutes to spare. Jake would be on time. He was good about that and after hearing about his helter-skelter childhood, she knew why. Routine would be comforting.

Jake's story had touched her. Kate's description of *healing his tortured soul* wasn't far off. But just because it sounded like a tired cliché didn't mean it never happened. Concepts became clichés because they were true.

Besides, the Brotherhood thought Jake was redeemable. She'd forgotten to mention that to Kate. Her roommate held those cowboys in high esteem. She did, too. They wouldn't leave Jake to flounder through this experience.

His truck pulled up outside the cottage at seven on the dot. If she'd been with Kate on a normal outing with the group, she would have pulled on her jacket and stepped outside to save him from coming to the door.

But this was a date. She stayed put and waited for Jake's rap on the screen door. Opening it, she invited him in. "You smell delicious."

"Same old aftershave. Let me help you with your jacket." He slipped the jacket over her arms and settled it on her shoulders. "You smell delicious, too." His breath warmed her cheek.

"Same old perfume."

"I like it. I've always wanted to tell you, but that seemed like... overstepping."

She turned around and he was *right there.* Her breath caught. "We should go."

Heat flared in his eyes, but he stepped back. "We should. You must be starving. That wasn't a very big sandwich."

Her laugh was breathless. Flirty. "How much do you think I eat?" She grabbed a small purse and tucked it in her coat pocket.

"You have a healthy appetite." A hand pressed lightly at the small of her back, he ushered her out the door. "You don't pick at your food. I hate when someone does that."

"Makes sense." So much made sense, now. "You didn't mention where your parents live."

"Casper, Wyoming. At least a day and a half drive from here. More like two days. Which is how I like it."

She walked down the steps. "You ran away from home, didn't you?"

"Yes, ma'am. I had my truck and a little bit of cash. I considered a few other towns, but when I drove into Apple Grove and took a turn around the square, I decided this was the place."

"And you got a job at the Buckskin?"

"Not quite." He helped her into the truck. He'd left it running with the heater on, but that wasn't anything special. He always did that when the weather was cool and he was chauffeuring folks.

"I want to hear the story of how you ended up at the Buckskin. I can't believe I never asked you."

He smiled. "You didn't need to know." He closed the door.

But now she did. She needed to know everything about Jake Lassiter.

_10_

Made it. Jake rounded the truck and climbed behind the wheel. Twice today he'd left Millie's house without giving in to temptation. Hadn't been easy with no one else there. But once he kissed Millie, he might never stop.

Fastening his seatbelt, he turned down the volume on the country music station and pulled away from the cottage. "Warm enough?"

"Perfect, thanks."

He glanced at her. "First time alone in my truck."

"I know."

"What's Kate's opinion of this?"

"What makes you think I discussed it with her?"

"I didn't fall off the turnip truck yesterday, Millie."

She laughed. "Fair enough. She hated hearing about your background. Which reminds me, how much does Henri know?"

"Some. I didn't go into detail, but she asked about my family when she hired me. I didn't announce I was never getting married, if that's what you mean."

"Sort of. But naturally you wouldn't announce it. She didn't need to know."

"You're getting the idea."

"If you didn't hire on at the Buckskin first thing, did you work somewhere else in town?"

"Yes, but you haven't finished telling me what Kate thinks about us going out."

She hesitated. "She really likes you."

"But she's not crazy about us dating."

"She's... being protective of me. I gather her ex had issues and she thought she could help him. I don't know the details, but it didn't work out. She warned me to be careful."

"Good advice. Come to think of it, she claims she'll never marry again. That guy must have done a number on her."

"Sounds like it. She begged me to learn from her mistakes."

"Yet here you are, ignoring her advice, throwing caution to the winds."

"Shoot, yeah! You think I'd pass up a steak dinner at the Moose?"

He grinned. "Steak? Did I mention steak? I could have sworn I said burgers."

"No, you said *dinner*. And I'm sure you want to make a good impression on me, so I figured on getting steak with all the trimmings. Oh, and a big slice of apple pie a la mode for dessert."

"Mercenary little thing, aren't you?"

"You mentioned today that you're glad I have a healthy appetite, so I'm simply living up to your expectations."

"I see. Good thing I brought a wad of cash with me. I suppose you'll also expect me to tip the band so they'll play your favorite song."

"That would be lovely. Do you know what it is?"

"*Breathe*, by Faith Hill."

"How did you know that?"

"I asked Kate a while back."

"Why?"

"Just curious." He'd learned a lot by finding out that piece of information. The romantic song was drenched in sensuality. The words described a woman's emotions while making love.

If the song was Millie's favorite, it stood to reason that she wanted that kind of experience. At the time, he wouldn't have given himself a snowball's chance in hell of ever being a participant in that fantasy. His odds had improved, but he'd take nothing for granted. He would treat this new situation with utmost care.

"Do you have a favorite song?"

The question caught him off-guard. "Can't say I do. I like most everything by Tim McGraw and his duets with Faith are great. I'm a Kenny Chesney fan. Plenty of good songs out there. How do you pick one over all the rest?"

"It's the one that makes you tingle all over when you hear it. Happiness swells in your chest and you feel like the world is a beautiful place."

"I can't think of a song that does that for me." He glanced at her. Should he say it? Yeah, seize the moment. "But it's exactly how I feel when I look at you."

She sucked in a breath. "Are you serious?"

"Absolutely." Too bad the light from the dash was so dim. He loved it when her cheeks turned pink.

"You're not teasing?"

"No, ma'am. I mean every word."

"Nobody's ever... I've never had a compliment like that. Thank you."

"You're welcome. It's nice to be able to say it. I've thought it often enough."

"You know what? I don't care if we crash and burn. I'll remember that compliment for the rest of my life. This experiment is already working for me."

He smiled. "Good. Me, too."

"Now I'm flustered, though. I've lost my train of thought. Oh, I remember! Your first job in Apple Grove. What was it?"

"Washing dishes for Ben Malone at the Moose."

"Huh! Why didn't you apply at any of the ranches in town?"

"Because I was an eighteen-year-old kid who knew very little about horses."

"You weren't a cowboy?"

"Far from it. A couple of my high school friends had horses. I could ride, but I didn't know anything about ranch work. Henri and Charley taught me everything I know."

"But why did they hire you if you were clueless?"

"Ben asked them to. I arrived in the summer and camped out since I didn't have enough money to rent a place. When he discovered how I was living, he knew I couldn't survive in a cheap tent with winter coming on."

"And Henri and Charley gave you a bunk and taught you ranch work. That's awesome."

"The timing was good, too. They'd just added a kitchen to the bunkhouse and I volunteered to cook the meals for the wranglers. It was something I knew how to do, something I loved doing while I learned the ropes."

"Serendipity."

"Yep."

"But I just happened to think—what about tonight? Did you fix dinner before you came to get me?"

"Didn't have to. Everyone decided to get pizza before the movie."

"Oh, yeah. I forgot about the movie plan."

"Do you still want to see it sometime?"

"I do."

"Want to go tomorrow night?"

"Two dates in a row?"

"It's my fault you're not seeing it with either the gang or Teague." He took a breath. "Did you break that date?"

"Yes. I texted him right after you left."

The tension in his chest eased. "You don't have to tell me, but since I'll be seeing him over at Ed's, I'd like to know how—"

"He wasn't surprised. You were right that he was watching us on the dance floor. He said it didn't look like a brother/sister arrangement to him."

"I'm sure not. Now I feel sort of bad for the guy. I cut him off at the pass."

"You did, but he sounded resigned to the outcome."

"The fact is, I owe him one. The thought of you with him hit me like a cattle prod to the privates."

"Ouch."

"Yeah, it was painful. Nick accused me of being a dog in the manger. I wouldn't ask you out, but I snarled at the first guy who did."

"Which brought us to dinner and dancing at the Choosy Moose."

"So it did." He scored a diagonal parking spot on the street. A lot around back handled overflow, but he preferred one of these spots. "We've never walked into the Moose as a couple."

"That's true and this is Apple Grove. Folks will talk."

He switched off the motor. "But you said most of them have assumed we'd get to this point sooner or later."

"I think that's a good guess."

"Then, like Teague, they won't be surprised that it's finally happened." He unlatched his belt and opened his door. "Let me help you out. The gutter is—"

"Jake, I won't budge until you come around. I love having you help me out of your truck. It's one of the special moments I treasure when I'm riding with you."

"But it's such a small thing."

"Maybe so, but I—"

"Clearly I need to raise the bar." He flashed her a smile. "I have way more to offer than saving you from puddles in the gutter."

11

Jake's last remark was the kind of teasing comment that made Millie's blood race and her panties grow damp. *I have much more to offer.* Oh, Lordy, did she want to find out!

But she'd promised herself, and insisted to Kate, that nothing would happen tonight except a kiss. Or maybe, let's be honest, several kisses. She wouldn't let making out lead to sex, though.

Walking into the Choosy Moose as Jake's date was a different experience from arriving with the Buckskin crowd. Smiles and curious glances followed them as the hostess led them to a table for two by the dance floor. A boisterous group of cowboys occupied the booth she and her buddies usually claimed.

He helped her off with her coat. As he draped it over her chair and she took her seat, she almost pinched herself to make sure she was awake.

Patsy, a fiftyish woman who'd been a server at the Moose ever since Millie had started coming here, hovered nearby with menus in hand.

She'd worked the wedding reception the night before, too.

Jake took the other chair and smiled at Patsy. "Have you recovered from last night's craziness?"

"Aw, I didn't mind." Beaming, she handed them each a menu. "It's fun to see everybody dressed up and having a good time. I'm happy for Matt and Lucy."

"Me, too. How's that pup of yours doing?"

"Growing, getting into things. Cute as the devil." She pulled out her electronic order pad and glanced at them. "Special occasion?"

"You could say that." Jake winked at Millie. "The lady finally agreed to go out with me."

"Good call, Millie. He's a great guy."

"Yes, he is." And gallant. He'd made it sound as if he'd been waging a long campaign that had finally succeeded.

Patsy took their order. "The band should be back from their break any minute. It's a new group Ben's trying out. I think you'll enjoy dancing to their music. Unless you're all danced out after last night."

Jake laughed. "Heck, no. Tonight I have Millie all to myself. No fighting off the other guys. I plan to take full advantage of that."

"Excellent. I'll be right back with your apple cider." She hurried away as the band returned and picked up their instruments.

"You sure know how to make a girl feel special."

Leaning his forearms on the table, he gazed at her. "You are special. It's ridiculous how long I've tolerated this situation."

"What situation?"

"Always on my guard, making sure I didn't show my hand by dancing with you too often or holding you closer than I should. Meanwhile I monitored every cowboy who took you out on the floor in case they were inappropriate and I had to step in."

"My goodness. That sounds exhausting."

"It was. And it ends now." As the band played the intro to *This Kiss*, he leaned closer and lowered his voice. "Tonight you're with me, just me. If any other yahoo comes over and asks for a dance, I'm asking you to please turn him down flat."

"Of course."

He stood and held out his hand. "Care to dance, Millie?"

Warmth flooded through her. "I sure do." She put her hand in his strong, sure grip. Good thing he was holding her steady. Her rubbery knees weren't up to the job.

Silly. She'd danced with Jake dozens of times, maybe even hundreds, considering the many trips to the Moose.

He led her to the dance floor. "Are you okay?"

"Never better."

"You're quivering."

"Nervous excitement."

"Ah." He turned back to her, his eyes alight with eagerness. "It's a fast one. Want to wait for something slow?"

She shook her head. "Just don't let go of me."

"Oh, I won't." He twirled her out onto the floor.

She could usually anticipate his moves. Not tonight. He was going for fancy. But he was true to his word and never let go of her as he executed one complicated maneuver after another.

In her effort to keep up with him, she lost the nervousness that had given her the shakes. The band had a vocalist who sounded a lot like Faith Hill and belted out the lyrics with vigor. If Millie hadn't been focused on the delights of kissing before, the words of the song did the trick.

As for Jake, his carefree grin made her heart swell with joy. He was totally loose tonight, more relaxed with her than ever before, even when he'd been kidding around. Could it be that she'd never met the real Jake?

When the song ended, he pulled her in close. "I *loved* that." Then he kissed her. Not for long, but long enough to stun her into speechless wonder, long enough to discover that his mouth on hers was an amazing sensation. Drawing back, he smiled. "It was a song about kissing, after all."

She couldn't breathe, let alone talk. She had to settle for nodding.

"Let's go have some cider. Looks like our salads have arrived, too."

She nodded again. She'd turned into a bobble-head doll.

He didn't let go of her hand until she was safely seated at the table. She appreciated that. She wasn't entirely convinced she would have found it on her own.

He sat down with a contented sigh. "I haven't danced like that in years. No, that's not true. I've *never* danced like that."

She took a shaky breath. "Me, either."

"There's something I'd like to talk about and it feels like we should be holding hands." He moved his salad plate aside and extended his arm across the table.

"Okay." She met him halfway and he laced his fingers through hers.

He studied their clasped hands for a moment. Then he looked up, his gaze warm. "I startled you when I kissed you just now. I probably should apologize, but I—"

"It's fine." More than fine. Her lips still tingled and she couldn't stop looking at his mouth.

"I was craving a small taste, like when you get a tiny spoonful of ice cream at the Apple Barrel."

"How was it?"

Heat flashed in his eyes. "I want more." Then he took a deep breath. "That's why I did it here. I'm not going to forget myself in the middle of the Choosy Moose."

"But you might somewhere else?"

"Yes, ma'am. Kissing you has been an obsession of mine for... months. Today I realized it was going to happen for real. I debated kissing you before I left the house this afternoon."

"I wondered if you would."

"Too dangerous with all that privacy. Same thing when I picked you up tonight."

"You think we'll get carried away?" Her heartbeat had begun to settle a bit but now it was off to the races again.

"Maybe you won't."

She wasn't so sure. Not anymore.

He leaned closer. "But I... taking this step is leaving me feeling... not wild, exactly, but unleashed. It's a great feeling. Energizing. I just don't want to mess up."

"Like how?" As if she didn't know.

His voice dropped to a low, intimate murmur. "Making love to you too soon."

Whoa. That right there was a bedroom voice. "What's... too soon?"

"Tonight."

"I, um—" She cleared her throat. "Uh-huh."

"I'd like to hold off for a while, maybe a week or two, but I..." His fingers tightened. "What do you think?"

"Sorry. My brain's not working. Not even a little."

He blinked. Then he laughed and shook his head. "Oh, Millie. You're not making this any easier. It's a good thing I live in the bunkhouse and you have a roommate or we'd—"

"Two steak dinners, coming up! I—oh, sorry if I'm interrupting."

Jake released Millie's hand and sat back with a sheepish expression. "No worries, Patsy. We were just—"

"Having a moment." Patsy set down Millie's plate first, then his. "I think that's lovely. I know how it goes. Close friends take the plunge and it begins to look like a good idea."

Jake flashed her a smile. "So true."

So true? Surely that hadn't just come out of his mouth.

"I'd ask if either of you wants another mug of cider, but you haven't touched the first ones. Or your salad. I'll leave you to it. Signal if you need anything." She gave Jake a pat on the shoulder before she left.

Millie waited until she was out of earshot. "So true? Jake, she was implying that we might be considering marriage and just last night you said—"

"I know. But I wasn't going to tell her we were a long way from that decision."

"Why not?"

"Because it's not a gentlemanly thing to say. In fact, it would border on an insult, as if I have to think long and hard about it."

"But you would!"

"Assuming my brain is working." He met her gaze.

"That's why we should hold off."

"It's the smart thing to do. In theory. I thought we should talk about it and come up with a game plan, but..."

"But?"

"Talking about it has only made me want to do it."

"Then we won't talk about it."

"Too late. We already did."

"We won't anymore. Problem solved."

"I doubt it." He lowered his voice to that sexy murmur again. "I have this image in my head of you all flushed and your eyes sparkling because you're thinking about making love to me. You've all but admitted that you want this as much as I do. How am I supposed to forget that?"

"I don't know."

"Neither do I. Taking it slow is the right thing to do, but I'll be damned if I know how."

"I have an idea."

"What's that?"

"Let's eat our steaks. It's good for our brains and might strengthen our resolve."

"And if it doesn't?"

"We'll be burning a lot of calories. We'll need the fuel."

_12_

We'll need the fuel. No kidding. Jake took a drink of his apple cider to cool down. Didn't help much. Picking up his knife and fork, he cut into his steak. Looked delicious. So did the woman across the table.

Like an idiot, he'd invited Millie to a romantic and sensual evening involving warm, succulent food and plenty of opportunities for body contact. If he'd wanted to slow things down between them, he could have taken her bowling.

"How's your steak, buddy?"

He glanced up at the Choosy Moose's cook. Nobody knew how old Ezra was, but he'd been at the Moose forever. He stood five feet nothing and probably weighed a hundred pounds dripping wet.

Jake finished chewing and swallowed. "Amazing, as always, Ezra. You have that routine down pat—ask about the food while the customer has a mouthful."

Ezra chuckled and looked over at Millie. "He's right, you know. Cooks and servers do that to amuse ourselves. How's your steak, Millie?"

"Perfect, Ezra. You're the best cook within the town limits. Kate's the best one outside them."

"Hey!" Jake pretended indignation. "How about including me in that statement?"

"You're a terrific cook, Jake, but Kate has a much bigger repertoire."

"Yeah, okay. I'll grant you that." He glanced at Ezra, who had a twinkle in his eye. The game was on. "But nobody can touch me when it comes to chuck-wagon stew."

Ezra sighed right on cue. "That's the God's truth. Too bad I can't put it on the menu. The customers would love it."

"So take my recipe and call it Jake's Chuck-Wagon Stew." They'd had this discussion many times. It always ended the same.

"I never stick with any recipe. You know that. It'll have to be Ezra's Chuck-Wagon Stew."

"Suit yourself. But let me know if you change your mind. We'll work out a licensing agreement."

Ezra laughed and squeezed his shoulder. "When hell freezes over, buddy. Hey, it's good to see you guys. Patsy told me you were here on an official date. I had to come see for myself."

"It's an official date," Millie said.

"Glad to hear it. Could you do me a favor and drag this guy to the altar? I want grandchildren before I croak."

Millie's eyes widened. "You're Jake's—"

"It's an honorary title. I don't have any kids, so I appropriated Jake when he came to work here. I let him do some cooking. He owes me a couple of grandchildren. I'd prefer a boy and a girl."

"I see."

"I'm counting on you, Millie. But I'd better get back to my kitchen and work my magic. Let me know when the wedding is. I'll be there with bells on." He gave them each a military salute and headed off to his inner sanctum.

"He's right about the magic," Millie said. "The food here is terrific."

"That guy has a job for life. He's a genius in the kitchen. I knew a few things when I started, but he taught me a ton of stuff in the months I worked here. Technically I was a dishwasher, but Ezra let me cook. A lot."

"Was Patsy here then, too?"

"She was."

"How many others?"

"Quite a few. Turnover is small at the Moose. Ben's a good boss."

"Until you told me you used to work here, I thought everyone was friendly with you because you're friendly to them."

"There's that, too. Several came on after I left, but I make it a point to remember everyone's name."

"You're onto something there. When a ranch guest takes note of my nametag and uses my name, they'll get special treatment for the rest of their stay."

"Is that right, Millie Jones?" He put down his knife and fork so he could take a sip of his apple cider. "I took note of your name that first day and used it whenever possible. I don't recall any special treatment."

She rolled her eyes. "You got special treatment. I don't bonk you on the head with a mop, which is what you deserved for accusing me of being an international spy with an alias."

"You didn't deny it, either. Are you?"

"I'd tell you, but then I'd—"

"You'd have to kill me. That's a lousy incentive. I don't want to die on our first date."

"I'm not an international spy. My last name is Jones, same as my dad's."

"Ah, but is there any proof of this supposed father? Where is he?"

"He died ten years ago. Fast-acting cancer."

His chest tightened. "I'm sorry. You were what, eighteen?"

"Yep, barely out of high school. At least he saw me graduate." She glanced at him. "He was a good dad. A good husband. He and my mom were really happy together."

"Must have been rough for both of you when he died. Is she doing okay?"

Her gaze shifted away and she sighed. "A year or so later she married Stanley."

"You don't like him."

"I don't dislike him."

"Are you sure? Because you said his name like you were staring at dog doo on the sidewalk."

She laughed. "I suppose I did."

"I hope you never say my name that way."

"I wouldn't. You're the anti-Stanley."

"I don't know about that. Yesterday you called me a pain in the ass."

"Which at least makes you interesting. Stanley is the most monochromatic person I've ever met."

"Monochromatic?"

"Devoid of color. You know your bumper sticker? *Life would be boring without me*?"

He smiled. "Thanks for noticing."

"Stanley needs one that says *Life will be boring with me.* Except Stanley would never get a bumper sticker because that would be far too interesting."

"I guess the big question is whether your mom's fine with mister plain vanilla, no sprinkles."

"She seems to be. I haven't had a private chat with her in forever because he's always there. They do everything together."

"Boring things."

"Yes! On my last visit, I had lunch with them at their favorite fast food place and they spent the entire time debating whether to buy a two-slice or a four-slice toaster."

"And where do you stand on that question?"

"Nowhere. I don't care."

"Really? Because I can make a good argument for a rugged four-slice. Then again, a slender two-slice is—"

"Don't start." She grinned.

"A two-slice is elegantly minimalist, but a four-slice says *let's party*! I personally—"

"Jake…" She started laughing.

"But you gotta forget the four-slice unless you're a butter knife ninja. That fourth one will cool before you get to it." He loved making her crack up. "Oh! What about slot size?" He wiggled his eyebrows. "Thick for bagels, long for hot dog buns. Size matters."

"Stop!" She wiped her eyes with her napkin. "No more toaster talk."

"No more? You can't leave me hanging. Which kind did they get?"

"They insisted I had to go with them to buy the darned thing and it was a two-hour ordeal of comparison shopping. They finally ended up with the most basic two-slice model in the store."

"Will it handle bagels and buns?"

"No."

"They'll live to regret that."

"If they do, I'll hear all about it in excruciating detail on my next visit."

He gazed at her. "I'm sorry your mom is joined at the hip to a boring man."

"Me, too. I wanted to be enthusiastic about her choice, but compared to my vibrant dad, Stanley is a major let-down. On the other hand, I don't have to worry about my mom being lonely without me."

"See? Silver lining."

"It is. I've always been fascinated by the wild, wild West, but I was going to stick around because of her. After Stanley was entrenched, I decided to give the West a shot."

"Why Apple Grove?"

"My story's not nearly as exciting as yours. I didn't set out on a driving trip. I searched online."

"Which is smarter. Saves time and money."

"I didn't have a lot of either. Just the urge for something different, something bursting with creativity and color. This town is almost as appealing online as in person."

"The Chamber of Commerce has been working on that."

"They've done a great job. I liked what I saw and followed the Buckskin Ranch link. Henri was looking for someone to apprentice to Sue, who wanted to retire in a year. We emailed, I came out for an interview, and she hired me on the spot."

"I remember her telling me that she'd taken you on."

"Oh, yeah? What did she say?"

"*She has red hair and she's feisty. You'll like her.*"

Millie smiled. "She thought I was feisty?"

"She wasn't wrong. You've been giving me a hard time ever since we met."

"Because you were so full of yourself."

"I was not."

"Oh, come on, Jake. You were all *I'm one of the top wranglers. I'm cool.*"

"Way cool."

"See?"

"But I wasn't a top wrangler. Charley had that position. Then Seth and Matt. I wasn't very high on the totem pole."

"But you were senior to CJ, Rafe, Nick and Leo. I'm telling you, there was an attitude going on. And it irritated the heck out of me. It also turned me on."

"Oh, yeah?" He smiled. "Are you saying attitude turns you on?"

"Some guys can be cocky and sexy at the same time."

"Like me."

"Let's just say my feelings about you were ambivalent back then."

"But then you softened toward me. I know you did. You stopped giving me such a hard time. You agreed to dance with me at the Moose."

"Why wouldn't I want to dance with you? You're very good at it. And that was the other thing that earned you points. I struggled with the line dances and you stayed close by so I could follow you. That was extremely sweet."

"I'm a sweet guy."

"I think I've always known that. Something in your eyes told me there was more to Jake Lassiter than what showed on the surface."

He let that sink in. "I hope you're right."

"I hope so, too."

He smiled. "Your line was supposed to be *I know I'm right.*"

Her expression was adorably serious. "But I don't. That's what... that's what this is all about."

"Yes, it is." He glanced at her plate. "Are you finished?"

"Sure am. It was terrific."

"What if I give Patsy our dessert order and we hit the dance floor again?"

"About that dessert..."

"You want something else besides the pie?"

"I don't want dessert at all. Please have some if you'd like to, but I'm stuffed."

"I'm not set on having pie and ice cream. I can easily skip it."

"I thought I could put away a steak dinner and a decadent dessert, but I'll never make it through pie a la mode. Instead of eating a rich treat, I'd rather dance with you."

He stood and held out his hand. "Then by all means. If I've calculated right, this should be a slow one." And tonight, he could hold her as close as he wanted.

13

So far the band had featured a woman on the vocals, but as the intro to Kenny Chesney's *You Save Me* began, one of the guys stepped to the mic.

"Oh, yeah," Jake said. "I thought maybe we'd just stand in one spot and sway for a change, but we're gonna waltz, Millie. This is a great song."

"Maybe it's your favorite song." She moved into his arms.

Her hand clasped in his, he pressed gently on her back to bring her within an inch of his muscled chest. "Any song is my favorite when I'm dancing with you."

"Ah, Jake, you could turn a girl's head."

He glanced around the floor as he swept her into the first steps of the waltz. "Which girl? Point her out. I've always wanted to try that trick."

"This girl, doofus."

He brought his attention back to her and lifted his eyebrows. "Doofus? Is that any way to talk to a guy who bought you a steak dinner with all the trimmings?"

"You're right. That's a little harsh. I should have called you a goofball, instead."

"That's more like it." He held her gaze as he guided her through the graceful dance. "I think you're fond of goofballs."

"I am."

"Just like I'm fond of feisty redheads who may or may not be international spies."

"Would you like me to have a secret identity? Would that be exciting?"

"Sure would, but this ol' boy can't handle any more excitement than you're already generating."

"I'm not doing anything."

"So you say. You just ran your tongue over your bottom lip. How do you suppose that makes me feel?"

"Who knows?"

"I'll tell you. It makes me feel like kissing you again. When you're across the table from me, you're out of reach, but now I've got you in range."

"You can't kiss me at the end of this dance, too."

"Why not?"

"Doing it once is no big deal, but if you keep doing it—"

"You don't want me to kiss you again?"

"I didn't say that. I just think it'll be noticed."

"So what? Unless you really are an international spy and don't want to draw unwanted attention to your mysterious self."

"Well, there's that."

"You know, I do like this song, but I never paid much attention to the lyrics." He pulled her a little closer so his body brushed hers in the turn. "I need to clarify that I don't expect you to save me. Kenny Chesney can ask his lady to save him if he wants, but I'm not into that."

"Good."

"I would appreciate it, though, if you'll let me kiss you at the end of this song."

"Because the Moose is a safe zone?"

"Yes, ma'am. I'm doing my best to stay out of trouble tonight. Can't get into too much of it on the dance floor."

"Then all right. But not too long." Anticipation jacked up her heart rate.

"I'll do my best to keep it short. I can't promise to keep it sweet."

Oh, boy. The brief one he'd given her earlier had been enough to fry her circuits. As the song ended, he pulled her close. Cupping her face in both hands, he settled his mouth over hers. And took command.

His boldness stole her breath. This was no gentle invasion. He brought the heat. And she caught fire.

Clutching the back of his head, she opened to him. With a soft groan, he deepened the contact, shifted the angle, molded his mouth to hers.

Her surroundings dissolved. Kissing Jake gave her the magic she'd dreamed of, the passion she craved. *Don't stop.* When he gradually lessened the pressure, she whimpered and tried to pull him back.

He hummed with obvious pleasure, but he lifted his mouth from hers, anyway. His soft murmur feathered her damp lips. "Gotta quit."

"No."

"The band's playing. Folks dancing around us."

"'S'okay."

"Come here." He drew her into his arms and nestled her head against his chest as he began to move in time to the music.

She linked her hands behind the crisp collar of his shirt and breathed in the scent of his aftershave. "Got carried away."

"Uh-huh."

"Your heart's beating fast."

"Sure is." He guided her slowly around the floor. "You pack a punch."

"Think anyone noticed us?"

Laughter rumbled in his chest. "Guaranteed."

"Secret's out."

"Wasn't much of one, anyway."

"What now?"

"Not sure. Didn't request your song, yet."

"Nope."

"But… I'm reaching my limit, Millie."

She nestled against his aroused body. "I know." And she didn't care. Those things she'd said to Kate? Naïve ramblings of a woman who'd never been kissed by Jake.

"I should take you home."

Lifting her head, she looked up at him. "What time is it?"

"Early, and I'd meant to stay longer, dance more, but—"

"Then let's go."

"Now?"

"Now. No point in torturing ourselves more."

"You're right." He released her and wrapped an arm around her shoulders as he escorted her off the floor.

His signal to Patsy brought her over to the table. "We'd like the check, please."

"You bet." She gave him a knowing look. "I'll be right back."

He gazed after her. "She thinks we're rushing off to—"

"She does, but if we try to explain, we'll only make it worse. Do you care if she has the wrong impression?"

He helped her on with her coat. "Not really. It's the right impression, in a way. And sooner or later, she'll be absolutely on target."

A delicious shiver traveled up her spine. "Is that a promise?"

He leaned down and his breath was warm as he murmured in her ear. "Yes, ma'am."

Arrows of heat ignited every combustible nerve in her body. "Good."

As he retrieved his jacket and hat from the back of his chair, Patsy returned with the check.

He handed her several bills.

"I'll fetch your change."

"No change."

"You're a generous man, Jake Lassiter." She turned to smile at Millie. "I'm happy for you two. I've known this guy for a lot of years, and I think he's finally got it right."

"Thanks." Millie met his gaze. "I think so, too. Ready?"

"Yes, ma'am." He ushered her out of the Moose and into his truck.

The chilly evening should have cooled her down, but sharing the cab with him had never been so charged with electricity.

As he backed out of the parking space, he glanced at the clock on the dash. "It's only a little past nine. Can't remember the last time I left the Moose this early."

"Because we're always here with the gang."

"Right. I doubt they're even back from the movie yet."

"Probably won't be for another hour or so." Pulse racing, she waited for him to pick up his cue.

"I wasn't planning on going inside with you, anyway, but now I definitely won't."

He was sticking with the program. Not surprising. She let some time go by and allowed the low volume of the country music station to fill the silence.

He glanced her way. "You're being quiet over there."

"I've been thinking. Are we being ridiculous?"

"Meaning?"

Pulse racing, she pushed on. "Is having sex now really going to ruin our chance at building a solid relationship?"

"That's the way I've heard it. And that's when two people have no major issues. Add in my background, and we're doomed unless we take it slow, get to know each other before we—"

"But we *do* know each other. We've been co-workers for years and friends for almost that long. Shouldn't that make a difference?"

"You probably can't ask that question of a man whose Wranglers are pinching his privates."

"Maybe I'm asking because my panties are damp."

He groaned. "No fair, Millie."

"Sure it is. If you can talk about your pinched privates, which I was quite aware of on the dance floor, by the way, I can mention my damp panties." She sucked in a quick breath. "Which are getting damper by the minute."

"My fault. I shouldn't have kissed you."

"I'm glad you did. Saved me the trouble of kissing you."

"You were planning to kiss me tonight?"

"Absolutely. You're not the only one who's been fantasizing about that activity. I was determined to get at least one kiss out of this date."

"Well, you got two, which was probably one too many, because now—"

"Now I realize that there's no way we're going to drag out this process, Jake. I'm a smoking volcano, and you're about to combust. If we're alone for five minutes, we'll—"

"That's why I'm not coming in."

"Then are you going to avoid being alone with me until you decide it's time?"

"Maybe."

"Think that through. How will it work?"

"Simple. We'll go on dates, like to the movies and bowling and stuff, and I'll bring you home, but I won't come in, especially if Kate's not there."

"No more mouth-to-mouth contact?"

"I, um, that's a good question. I didn't factor in how—"

"Uh-huh. Now you're getting the idea. Those kisses lit the fuse and it's gonna keep burning whether we're at the movies or in the bowling alley or having lunch at Gertie's Café."

"You're saying we'll live in a state of perpetual frustration."

"Yes, but only if we avoid another lip-lock." She swallowed. "I predict we're only one kiss away from igniting the stick of dynamite in your Wranglers."

<u>14</u>

"You're right." Jake made the turn onto the ranch road and steered around the muddy spot left by the last downpour. "Kissing you gets me hot. I wasn't planning on doing it again tonight."

"But you want to." The breathy, seductive note in Millie's voice was likely no accident. She was on her high horse about this issue.

"Of course I *want* to, but that doesn't mean—"

"You'll want to the next time you see me, too."

"That's a given."

"The second time was more intense than the first. The third time will be even more—"

"Not necessarily."

"Speak for yourself. I can hardly wait for our next kiss. It'll be a doozy."

She was right about that, too. He could already taste it. "Here's the thing. Every relationship I've had with a woman has begun with sex. I want us to be different."

"How long had you known these other women before you ended up in bed with them?"

"Not long. That's what I'm saying. Sex was the glue that kept us involved with each other."

"Then we *are* different. If we ended up in bed together, it would be after years of knowing each other. It wouldn't be what holds us together."

"But this is our first date."

"I'll admit that's how I was looking at it today. I even told Kate that we wouldn't be doing anything tonight because it was too soon."

"See? I'm not the only one who thinks—"

"Then you kissed me. Twice."

"Again, my mistake."

"Like I said before, we would have kissed tonight. I would have seen to it. And I doubt we would have ended with one. You don't get to take the blame for this predicament."

"But I've been guilty of magical thinking. I imagined we could date like normal people do." He cruised past the ranch house. Judging by the lights on downstairs, Henri was still up. She could see the front of the cottage from her window. No matter. He wasn't staying.

"We're not normal people."

That made him laugh.

"Well, we're not! We didn't meet at some event and exchange phone numbers. We didn't start out having a coffee date, then progress to a lunch date and finally go for the big dinner date."

"Truthfully, I've never done it like that."

"I have, and it's kinda boring. Like you're following some formula. Oh, and FYI, by the dinner date, it's fairly common to consider having sex."

"It is?"

"So by that criteria, we're due. And we find ourselves with a golden opportunity."

"Not exactly."

"Why?"

He parked in front of the cottage and left the engine running so the heat would stay on. Then he unsnapped his seatbelt and turned to her. "I chose not to bring condoms."

"Kate and I figured you wouldn't."

"You talked about it?"

"Of course. She said if I wanted to bring you in anyway, she'd wear earplugs."

"Dear God."

"But she's not here, so we can carry on as much as we want."

He gazed at her in the dim light from the dash. The prospect she offered made him dizzy with longing. "Last night I gave myself zero chance of ever making love to you."

"And tonight, if I remember the movie times right, we can have about an hour alone to explore the possibilities. Maybe we can't make love the traditional way, but there are so many—"

"I'm aware." His voice rasped. He cleared his throat. "And I want to, Millie. You've made your case."

She unlatched her belt, too. "Then shut off the motor and we'll go in."

"I'm not going in with you."

"Why not?"

"Because the first time I make love to you, I don't want to be watching the clock. We'd have to check the website and make sure we know exactly when that show is ending. Then we'd have to set the alarm on one of our phones so I'd be gone before Rafe brings Kate home."

"Or not. She'll see your truck and know what's going on. We're all adults. It's no big—"

"It is to me. I've thought about this, too, and I figured if we took it slow, I'd have time to figure out when and where we'd make love the first time. I want it to be special."

"That's very sweet." She drew in a deep breath. "And touching. Are you saying you want to take a raincheck for a more appropriate time and place?"

"Something like that. I don't have anything in mind yet, but I'll work on it."

"Can you please work on it fast?"

"Trust me, I'll give it my full attention."

"Were you thinking of the Apple Grove Hotel?"

"No."

"It's old, but it's elegant. I've never stayed there, but—"

"The walls are paper thin."

"Oh. You've taken someone else there."

"Right."

"Forget the hotel, then. It would only be a solution for one night, anyway." She turned to face him. "How did you manage a relationship with your other girlfriends? Besides the hotel, I mean."

"They had their own places."

"So do I. And Kate is very easy to get along with."

"I know she is. But I don't... it feels like bush league. Like we should be past that."

"But we each share living quarters."

"We do, and mine's even more complicated a venue than yours."

"Yeah, no. The bunkhouse is a non-starter."

"I wouldn't ask you to do that even if they were all gone. That's bush league squared." Reaching for her hand, he laced his fingers through hers. "I'll figure this out." Then he gave her hand a squeeze and released it. "I'll walk you to the door."

"Okay."

He left the motor running, grabbed his hat from the dash and opened his door.

"Don't you want to shut that off?"

"No, ma'am." He put on his hat. "It's my insurance policy."

"To keep you from going in with me, after all?"

"Uh-huh."

"That soothes my ego."

"Glad to be of service." Climbing out, he shut the door, rounded the truck and helped her down.

"Sure you don't want to turn off that motor?"

"Not when mine's going full throttle." He closed her door. Keeping her hand in his, he started toward the porch steps.

"You're lucky I'm not a devious woman."

"You're not?" He climbed the steps and focused on the soft rumble of his truck's engine. One kiss. One. Then he'd be back in that truck.

At the door, she turned to him. "If I'd wanted to sabotage you, I would have unbuttoned my blouse while I was sitting in the truck and given you a peep show before I shut off the motor and pocketed the keys."

He stared at her. "Holy hell, Millie."

"Would it have worked?"

"Like a charm. Why didn't you?"

"Do you wish I had?"

"Not answering that." Nudging back his hat, he pulled her close. "One kiss."

"Make it a good one."

"Don't worry." He lowered his head. "It'll be a doozy." He touched down.

And was lost. Her mouth... dear God, he couldn't get enough of her supple lips. He delved deeper, reveling in her moist heat, the wicked stroke of her tongue, the erotic pressure when she sucked on his.

Her coat was unbuttoned. His, too. When had that happened? Who cared? He pulled her in tight and she wrapped one leg around his, opening to him, inviting him to rock forward... sweet agony... *Millie.*

She moaned and reached for the buttons on his shirt. He had one of hers undone and had reached for the next one when the nearby hoot of an owl startled him.

CJ. That crazy guy had perfected the call of a great horned owl. Jake lifted his head, breathing hard.

"Owl." Millie gazed up at him, her eyes heavy-lidded with passion. "Come back here, you."

"Might be CJ."

"It isn't. They're still—"

"Yeah." He took a ragged breath. "At the movies." He gazed into her flushed face. "If I don't go now, I won't go at all."

"I'll wait while you turn off the motor."

He shook his head and took another lungful of air. "I'm leaving."

"Your body wants to stay." She pressed her palm against his chest. "Your heart's going a mile-a-minute."

"I know. And I ache for you, but I want all night, with no threat of being interrupted in the middle of... anything. Let's wait for that, Millie. Please."

She cupped his face in both hands. "Okay, but don't make us wait too long."

"I'll get something worked out for tomorrow night."

"Promise?"

"Yes." Somehow he'd do it.

"Then take off, cowboy." She stepped back. "Sweet dreams."

"I know exactly what kind of dreams I'll have. And they won't be sweet. Good night, Millie."

"Good night, Jake."

Touching two fingers to the brim of his hat, he turned and clattered down the steps. Wearing new jeans tonight had been a mistake. No give to them at all.

She was still standing by the door when he got in the truck and looked out the window. He blinked the lights and revved the engine.

Blowing him a kiss, she went inside. Then she flicked the porch light on and off.

Tapping the horn lightly, he put the truck in reverse, backed out of the small parking area and drove away.

To his surprise, the trucks were parked by the bunkhouse and judging from the boisterous sounds coming from inside, a poker game was in progress. The movie must have let out earlier than Millie had calculated. Was Kate in there?

He walked in and everyone looked up from the game to stare at him.

Kate was the first to speak. "What are you doing here?"

"I live here."

"Where's Millie?"

"At your house."

Rafe started laughing. "All that for nothing."

"All what?"

"It's like this," Nick said. "We got out of the movie earlier than expected and decided to head over to the Moose to spy on you and Millie. Patsy informed us you'd left."

Leo folded his cards and laid them face down. "Assuming you'd gone back to the cottage for some quality time we invited Kate over for some poker."

"Actually, I invited myself. Didn't want to interrupt and all that."

"Oh."

"Yeah, *oh*." Kate shook her head. "Why aren't you—" Her eyes widened. "Don't tell me you had a fight."

"No fight. We had a great time." He noticed Kate wasn't the only woman in residence. Serena was also at the table. Not Isabel, though. CJ was missing, too. "Where's CJ? And Isabel?"

"Over at Isabel's cabin," Kate said. "Some people seize the moment and others don't. I can't believe you're not with Millie."

"She invited me in, but—"

Rafe's loud groan cut him off. "She invited you in and you turned her down? Major mistake, bro. Huge."

"I didn't like the odds of Kate coming home in the middle of the action."

She glanced at him. "But as you can see, I took steps to keep that from happening."

"I didn't know that. You could have come straight home."

"And noticed your truck was there. I would have asked Rafe to bring me over here for a while to give you two some space."

"But I couldn't count on that and I didn't want to start out worrying about such things. The first time should be special."

Kate's expression gradually softened. "Ah, now I see the problem. You're way more romantic than I've given you credit for."

He shrugged, embarrassed. "Normally I'm not."

"Except when it comes to Millie." Rafe gave him a knowing look.

"Guess so."

Kate gazed at him. "Now that I understand, I have a solution for you. And I think you'll love it."

15

Kate's text added one more element of wonkiness to a wild and crazy evening. *I'm at the bunkhouse playing poker with the guys and Serena. I'm winning so I plan to stay awhile. You're welcome to drive over if you want, or someone can come fetch you. If not, see you in the morning.*

Millie texted back that she was settling in with a cup of herbal tea and a book. She wasn't about to go over there. The night had been enough of a rollercoaster without adding poker night with the gang. And Jake.

The tea and book routine made her drowsy, thank goodness. A night of tossing and turning might not be in her future, after all. She went to bed and was asleep before Kate came home.

When she woke up the next morning, her roommate had already left for the dining hall to cook breakfast for the guests. Millie showered and dressed, fixed herself some breakfast, and set off to make the rounds of the cabins.

She shifted her routine to arrive at Seth and Zoe's cabin first. They were checking out this morning and she didn't want to miss saying goodbye.

Zoe called out a greeting when Millie rapped on the door.

"It's me." Millie poked her head in.

"Hey, you." Once again, Zoe was alone with Hamish, getting him dressed for the trip home. "Seth's down at the barn. His replacement, Garrett something-or-other, just arrived from Wyoming." She pulled a long-sleeved shirt over the baby's head. "Seth wants to meet him since he's the first new guy hired in about nine years. It's a big deal."

"It sure is. Leo's the most recent hire, and he was here when I came on board. I wonder how the Brotherhood will handle having a new wrangler in the bunkhouse. Of course they'll make him feel welcome, but...."

"There's the Brotherhood thing." Zoe worked Hamish's pudgy arms into the sleeves of the shirt.

"Right. This guy wasn't here when Charley was alive. Or Seth's mom. Do you know how old he is?"

"Twenty-seven." She picked up a baby-sized pair of faux Wranglers with snaps strategically placed for easy diaper changes.

"That's a lot older than the others were when they came."

"Yeah, Seth expected Henri to hire another teenager who needed a place to land." She tugged the pants over the baby's diapered bottom.

"He said that was her pattern when Charley was alive."

"She does do that. Or did. People change."

Zoe glanced over her shoulder and smiled. "Like Jake? I heard you guys went out on your first-ever date last night."

"We did." Millie's cheeks warmed. "Listen, do you need any help getting packed? Or can I hold Hamish while you get organized?"

"You can definitely hold Hamish." She grabbed soft booties that looked like boots and put them on the baby's feet. Then she handed him over.

Millie accepted the sweet-smelling baby and cradled him in her arms. "Looks like you're destined to be a cowboy, buddy." He gazed up at her with interest and waved his tiny fists. "Cute outfit, Zoe."

"Thanks." She folded the blanket Hamish had been lying on and tucked it into a tote sitting nearby. "Did you have fun on your date?"

"We had fun. Jake's... well, he's Jake."

Zoe laughed. "I'm just getting to know the guy, but I understand what you mean. I love the bumper sticker on his truck—*Face it, life would be boring without me.*"

"That's him in a nutshell." And yet, was it? He didn't fit inside a nutshell, or a bumper sticker. There was so much more to him.

"For what it's worth, Seth is excited about you and Jake. He wondered if you'd eventually get together."

"I wouldn't say we're exactly together, yet."

"Heading in that direction, then."

"Cautiously. We're both taking a risk. For one thing, we work together."

"That makes it trickier." Zoe gathered several plush toys and began filling a second tote. "Although Seth is convinced everything will turn out great."

"That would be lovely." She leaned down and gave Hamish a kiss on his soft cheek. "I'll miss you guys."

"Same here. I'm glad the wedding brought us up to the Buckskin. Seth loves Eagles Nest and his newly-discovered relatives there, but this is where he grew up. We'll be back. Soon, I hope."

"I hope so, too."

"Listen, do you need to start cleaning? I can scoot out of the way if you—"

"I don't have to clean now. Most of the guests are leaving today because they came for the wedding like you did. Not that many are checking in, so I can take my time working through the cabins. I just wanted to say goodbye."

"I'm so glad you did. We have each other's cell phone numbers, so keep in touch. Let me know what's happening with Jake."

She handed the baby back to Zoe. "And send me pictures of this little guy. If I can't hold him every day, at least I want to see his adorable face."

"I promise to do that."

"Safe travels." Millie hugged her and left. She was used to goodbyes. She lived on a guest ranch where nice people came, bonded with the staff, and left. But Seth, Zoe and baby Hamish weren't guests. They were family.

Her next stop was Isabel's cabin. Her flight was several hours before Serena's, so Millie wanted to touch base. She tapped on her door.

"Door's open! Come on in."

Millie left her supplies outside and went in. "I was hoping to catch you."

Isabel zipped her suitcase and set it on the floor. "I was about to put this outside the door for CJ. He's taking me to the airport. Should be here any minute."

"Then I made it just in time. I just wanted a chance to say it was great getting to know you. I hope you come back soon."

"Oh. That's so sweet of you. I'd love that. I've had a fabulous time."

A truck pulled up outside and Millie glanced out the partially open door. "That's CJ. Have a safe trip home."

"Thanks so much." Isabel gave her a hug, picked up her suitcase and hurried out the door.

Millie waited until CJ's truck pulled away before she retrieved her supplies and dived into her morning's work.

Although she'd told Zoe she had all day to clean, she decided to get 'er done in one fell swoop, which meant working through her lunch hour. Jake wouldn't approve, but Jake wasn't here.

But then he showed up as she closed the door on her last cabin. He walked toward her with his trademark grin, the one that had stolen her heart a long time ago, much longer than she'd admitted to him.

She returned his smile. "How did you find me?"

"Just surveyed the area looking for the mop bucket. How come you didn't answer my text?"

"You texted?" She pulled out her phone. "So you did. Sorry. Must've come in when I was vacuuming."

He stopped when he was about four feet away and nudged back his hat. "Might be best if I communicate from here."

"Did you come down with something?"

"Yes, ma'am. A bad case of craving Millie Jones."

"I see."

"Another two steps closer and we'd have a public display of affection going on. Not classy in broad daylight in the guest area of the ranch."

"I agree."

"You sure look pretty with the sunlight on your hair."

"You sure look manly with your boots all muddy and your sleeves rolled back."

"Been helping Nick replace some fencing in the pasture. Need to get back to it, but... have you talked to Kate?"

"Not today."

"Damn. I was hoping you had."

"Why?"

"I figured it'd be better if you heard the plan from her. Then you could think on it before you and I talked about it."

"The plan for what?"

He glanced around. "What we discussed last night."

Her heart began to pound. "You mean..."

"Yes, ma'am."

"What's the plan?"

"It's, um... oh, shoot, there's my phone." He pulled it out of his pocket and started backing away. "Listen, I should go. Nick probably needs me to... I should go."

"I didn't hear your phone ring."

"Talk to Kate." Touching two fingers to his hat brim, he turned and left, his long strides taking him quickly away.

She opened her mouth to call him back before he was out of range. Closed it again. He likely wouldn't stop, anyway. His phone hadn't rung. She'd bet on it.

Whatever the plan was, he wanted her to get the news from Kate. He'd looked worried, as if she might reject the idea, whatever it was. Fat chance. She couldn't wait to spend quality time with that sexy cowboy.

_16_

Jake figured he'd hear from Millie before too long. Luckily he didn't have barn duty tonight. He'd spent his lunch hour making a huge pot of chili and baking cornbread. Maybe he'd be eating chili and cornbread with the Brotherhood tonight and maybe he wouldn't. Depended on Millie.

Garrett Whittaker, the new hire, was spending his first night in the bunkhouse. Jake's urge to be hospitable warred with a far more powerful urge.

Given the option, he'd choose Millie. But she might not go for Kate's plan, at least not all of it. He wouldn't blame her for hesitating.

He finished up the work in the pasture and hit the showers. By the time he came out, he had a text from Millie. *Kate's left for the dining hall. Can you come over to talk?*

Be there in ten. He dressed in record time, hopped in his truck and drove to the cottage.

She opened the door before he had a chance to knock and jumped right to the heart of the matter. "How do you feel about this plan?"

He walked in and closed the door behind him. "How do you feel about it?"

"I asked you, first."

He glanced around the room as if seeing it for the first time. "I've never spent an entire week with a woman. It'd be a big step. At least for me."

She nodded. "That's what I thought. And there's your job cooking for the guys. I know that means a lot. To you and to them."

"I mentioned that last night when Kate came up with this, and you should have heard Rafe, Nick and Leo carry on. *We'll handle it. Take that week with Millie. Don't be an idiot.* And so forth. They want us to do this. A bunch of matchmakers."

She smiled. "That's very cute, but if the concept stresses you out..."

"I won't lie. It does."

"We could dial it back to just one night. Henri and Kate are totally flexible. Henri agreed to set Kate up in her spare room for the week, but I could help Kate bring her stuff back tomorrow. No big deal."

"Would that work better for you?"

She gazed at him. "I don't want to freak you out, but if you left it up to me, I'd want you to stay the whole week."

His chest tightened. "All right."

"I'm not sure it *is* all right with you."

He took off his hat and ran his fingers through his hair. "It's just that... it gives me plenty of time to mess up."

"Mess up how?"

"Easy." He sighed. "I'll say something wrong, do something you don't like. You'll call me on it and I'll turn into my father."

"That's a huge assumption. Besides, you've lived with the guys in the bunkhouse for years. Have you turned into your father over there?"

"No, because it's a totally different environment. One of us develops an attitude, the others cut him down to size. Nothing gets completely out of hand because at least one of us steps in as a peacemaker."

"And think of all you've learned through that process." She moved closer, her flowery scent teasing him with the possibilities. "At first I didn't want to stress you with this plan, but now I wonder... maybe it's time to find out you're not your father."

He became lost in the emerald depths of her gaze. He sucked in a breath. "Just so you know, you could talk me into this, no problem. When you get that look in your eyes, I'm your slave. But you could be asking for big trouble."

"Or I could be asking for a sexy cowboy in my bed for the next week. What red-blooded woman wouldn't want that?"

He reached for her, couldn't help it. Touching her grounded him as nothing else could. "I just want you to know that by testing this, you're pressing on my weak spot. I planned to approach it more gradually."

"And make love maybe sometime in the next month or so?"

"Yeah, that was never going to work." He drew her closer. "The one part I like about Kate's plan is that we can make love tonight."

"And every night for the next week."

"I'm not counting my chickens." He tossed his hat in the general direction of the couch. "But I like my chances for the next twelve hours." Claiming her mouth, he surrendered to the urge that had been taunting him ever since he'd stepped through the door.

She responded with enthusiasm and his misgivings vanished in the heat of her kiss. She believed in him—way more than he believed in himself. He'd cling to that. As he plundered her mouth and she gave as good as she got, he couldn't wait to begin this week of discovery. It could end in disaster. In the meantime, he'd treasure every moment with this amazing woman.

* * *

Agreeing to a romantic week with Millie meant Jake had things to do and places to go. It was the only motivation strong enough to get him out of that cozy cottage. Tearing himself away from her hot kisses took willpower, but he needed to shop for food. Instead of cooking for the Brotherhood this week, he'd be cooking for her. He promised to be back by six with dinner fixings and his gear.

When he pulled in at two minutes before six, smoke drifted from the chimney. Fire suited his mood perfectly. Excitement hummed in his veins as he unloaded a duffle stuffed with a week's worth of clothes, a bottle of champagne and the grocery bag with the perishables in it. He'd come back for the other grocery bag and two six-packs of cider.

She walked out on the porch in an outfit he'd never seen, wide-legged pants and a loose shirt in dark green velour. She wore furry moccasins on her feet. "Can I help?"

"Sure." Setting down his duffle and the champagne, he held onto the bag of groceries and cupped the back of her head. "I could really use a kiss."

"On the porch?"

"On my mouth." He leaned over and captured her smiling lips. Ah, so good. Better keep his wits about him, though, or he'd drop the groceries. This bag had the eggs, and the market was closed.

Reluctantly lifting his head, he gazed into her luminous eyes. "Honey," he murmured, "I'm home." He'd intended it as a joke, but it had come out sounding way more meaningful than that.

"How does it feel?" The pink light of sunset bathed her face in a rosy glow.

"Terrific. What's this you have on?"

"A lounging outfit."

"Is it new? I've never—"

"I've had it, but I only wear it when I'm... well, lounging."

"Is that what we'll be doing?"

"Sometimes." Her eyes sparkled. "I mean, we can't always be—"

"Why not?"

She laughed. "So that's how it's going to be."

"That's how it's going to be. But first I'll feed you. You'll need the fuel." He stepped back and handed her the bag of groceries. "I'll go fetch the rest."

"Wow, this is heavy. How much did you buy, anyway?"

"A few days' worth," he called over his shoulder. "I'll have to shop again to get us through." He grabbed the other bag. The bouquet he'd chosen was tucked on top, a burst of festive color. First bouquet he'd ever purchased for a woman.

He picked up the cider and headed for the porch. The champagne bottle was gone, so she must have snagged it before going in. Leaving his duffle for now, he walked into the house.

Talk about fire power. From the logs blazing in the fireplace to the candles flickering on nearly every surface in the living room, the place was glowing with warmth and energy. "Love the candles," he called out as he walked toward the kitchen.

"Me, too." She met him at the doorway. "I—oh, Jake. You brought flowers."

"Only because I found a bouquet with no red roses in it. I like flowers, just not that specific one."

"Well, these are beautiful. Thank you." She relieved him of the bag. "I'll put the flowers in water. Just stick the cider in the fridge."

He found a spot for it. "I'll get my duffle and that'll be it." He brought it into the house. Now what? He'd never been in her bedroom, although he knew which one was hers. "Where would you like me to put—"

She came out of the kitchen carrying a white vase with the flowers in it. "I'll show you." She set the flowers on a small table behind the couch. Two chairs from the kitchen stood on either side and she'd added placemats, napkins and silverware.

"Was that table always there?"

"It was over by the window. I moved it so we can eat and enjoy the fire."

"Nice."

"Come on back. I cleared some space for you."

He followed her down the hall. "You didn't need to do that. I can just keep everything in my duffle."

"You could, but that makes it easier for you to clear out if we get crossways with each other."

"Aha! You think we will, too."

"Not at all. We'll have a lovely time." She led him into her bedroom, walked to the dresser and pulled out the top drawer. "You can have this for your underwear."

"Okay." Her comment barely registered. He was too busy staring at the bed. "I didn't know you had a king."

"Crazy, I know. It's too big for the room, but when I went shopping for a bed, this was only a little more than the queen and I loved the rustic look of the headboard. I thought, why not? The frame will last me a lifetime."

"It's…" He took a shaky breath. "I can see why you'd…" He was babbling, so he stopped talking until he could get his bearings. The beautifully carved headboard and the wide expanse of mattress covered by a multi-colored quilt constituted his ultimate bed fantasy.

"I've had it about two years and I love it. Sue left me her double bed when she moved out, but I always knew I'd replace it when I had the money."

"You did well." He kept his distance from her, although he couldn't keep his distance from the bed. One kiss and they'd be on it. He wanted to lead up to making love, not grab her within fifteen minutes of his arrival.

"This is my dream bed. Hope you like it."

"I do."

She gave him a quick glance.

He shrugged. "Anyone would."

17

If Millie stayed in that room much longer, she'd tackle Jake. Not cool. She slid open the closet door. "Plenty of hangers and space for the rest of your clothes. Kate took her lotions and potions out of the bathroom so you can put your toiletries in there."

"Thanks." His chest heaved. "Appreciate you both making room for me."

"Of course. I'll leave you to it." Or she would after she squeezed past him. "Excuse me. Tight quarters."

He groaned. "You're killing me, lady."

"Right backatcha, cowboy. I'll start putting away the food." She hurried back down the hall. After rearranging the logs in the fireplace and adding another one, she returned to the kitchen and continued unloading the second bag.

She left the package of two filets out, guessing they were for tonight. He'd splurged on those, along with some pricey asparagus and out-of-season salad greens and cherry tomatoes.

He'd hit the grocery store's bakery case for cinnamon rolls for breakfast and an apple pie, supplied to the market by the Apple Barrel. She discovered the pint of vanilla ice cream before it started melting.

He'd even bought a package of butter. She had it in her hand when he walked into the kitchen. She held it up. "I have butter. We can use—"

"I'm partial to that brand."

"Isn't all butter the same?"

"Not to me. That one's amazing. I can taste the difference."

"Kate's discriminating, but she gets some generic brand."

"I'll bet she wouldn't if she once tried this. It's worth the expense."

She laughed. "I've never met a butter snob before."

"Well, now you have."

She swept a hand over the counter laden with groceries. "I didn't expect you to provide all the food. And I'll share the cooking chores."

"I don't think of cooking as a chore. It relaxes me. And—" He paused and dipped his head. "Huh."

"What?"

He glanced up. "My father doesn't cook. I never made the connection between that and my love for it. Mom cooks, but with zero enthusiasm."

"I've seen you in action. Major enthusiasm."

"And maybe I have dear old dad to thank for it, although he certainly didn't mean to do me a favor." He shook his head. "That's enough about him, though. I don't want to spend any more time talking about the guy."

"In any case, you've convinced me that cooking is your passion, and I—"

"One of my passions."

His direct gaze made her flush. "What I was about to say is—the kitchen is all yours. I'll try not to get in your way."

"That's no fun." He rolled back his sleeves and washed up at the sink. "Get in the way all you want. Kiss the cook often and deeply. It'll inspire me."

"I never thought of cooking as an erotic experience."

"No? I always have." He turned to her. "I didn't buy or bring spices. I was counting on Kate having—"

"She does. A bunch." She pulled out one of the under-counter drawers and stepped back to let him inspect the contents.

He studied the array of bottles like an artist choosing his color palette. After taking out several jars, he asked for a bowl and mixed up a concoction of olive oil, wine vinegar and various spices.

"Salad dressing?"

"Could be, but it's marinade for the steak. Now I need a small baking dish."

She pulled one out of a cupboard. "Like this?"

"Perfect." He unwrapped the steaks, tucked them in the dish and poured the contents of the bowl over them. "Normally I'd marinade them for much longer, let them get totally juiced up, but they only get a quickie tonight."

Right on cue, her body grew moist and achy. "You're a devil, Jake Lassiter."

"Just demonstrating the erotic nature of cooking, since you said it was a new concept."

"Not anymore."

"I need to pay attention to these asparagus stalks, now."

"I'm hesitant to ask what you're planning to do to them."

"Got a steamer?"

"Yes." She dug in a bottom cupboard and found it.

"These stalks are stiff and unyielding. But a little warm steam and they'll surrender, becoming supple. A drizzle of virgin olive oil and a light dusting of spices and they're ready for the heat from the broiler and the climactic moment when they'll burst with flavor."

"This is the most X-rated cooking demonstration I've ever seen. How many times have you gone through this routine?" *With other women?*

"Never."

"Never?"

He smiled. "I'm a ham, Millie. All you had to say was *I've never thought of cooking as an erotic experience.* I was off to the races."

"You made all this up just now?"

"Yes, ma'am. Got a kiss for the cook?"

She sashayed over to him and grabbed the front of his shirt with both hands. "I want to rip the clothes from your body and have my way with you on the kitchen floor."

"That's what I like to hear." He pulled her close and kissed her until her panties were drenched and she was gasping for air.

She drew back a fraction of an inch. "Come to bed with me. Now."

"I thought you'd never ask." Without preamble, he scooped her up and carried her out of the kitchen. "Steak needs more time in the marinade, anyway."

"Not me." She was giddy with excitement and the glorious rush of unchecked desire. She'd lost one moccasin when he picked her up and she kicked off the other one. "I'm juicy and tender. Bring on the heat."

"Oh, I'll be bringing it, Millie-girl. I've waited a long time for this." He carried her through the door of her bedroom.

"You left on the bedside light."

"Yes, ma'am. And turned down the covers."

"No way."

He laid her on the cool sheet, proving his point. "If you're going to leave me alone in your bedroom, I'm going to set it up the way it needs to be when the time comes."

Two condoms lay on the nightstand. "You're incredible."

"Thanks for noticing." He braced a hand on the nightstand and pulled off his boots. "I have a strong suspicion you're naked under that outfit."

"Would I do that?"

"God, I hope so."

"Guess you'll have to find out."

His blue eyes darkened to navy. "I estimate I'll make that discovery in about thirty seconds." Straightening, he began stripping out of his clothes. His shirt and T-shirt went flying.

He was mouth-wateringly beautiful. In the heat of a summer day he'd often peel off his shirt when he was working, fueling her fantasy of someday caressing his sculpted body. That day had arrived. She left the bed.

He paused, his hands at his belt buckle.

She met his hot gaze. "Can I do something first?"

"What?"

"This." She placed a hand on either side of his neck, stroked across his broad shoulders and down the swell of his biceps. "Your skin's hot."

"So's the rest of me." His voice fell into the low, sexy range that gave her the shivers.

Smoothing her palms over his muscled forearms, she grasped his hands and lifted them to her shoulders. "I've dreamed of touching you this way."

"I've dreamed of touching you *every* way."

"I want you to." She caressed his firm pecs, pausing to absorb the rapid thud of his heart. "But first..." She slid her hands over his abs and reached for his belt buckle.

Unfastening it, she drew his belt through the loops, taking her time. She let it drop to the floor. Her heart thrummed with excitement as she undid the metal button of his jeans and worked the zipper down.

He gasped. "Millie..."

"Before you get suited up..." She dragged in a breath. "I'm dying to get my hands on you."

His chest heaved. Then he shoved down his jeans and briefs and kicked them away. "By all means."

18

Good thing he'd perfected the art of restraint where Millie was concerned. He'd need every ounce of it. The moment she wrapped her warm fingers around his aching cock, the urge to climax hit him hard.

He fought it. He was stunned that she wanted to touch him, that she'd interrupted the action so she could do it. He closed his eyes and vowed he wouldn't come. Her intimate caress felt like heaven. Holding back was hell.

"Thank you." She let go and backed away.

He opened his eyes. "You're thanking *me*?"

"Oh, yeah." She was breathing fast as she gave him a once-over. "You and whatever planets aligned to bring you here tonight." Her eyes glowed. "The image of you standing in my room gloriously naked and aroused is mine forever. The tactile memory, too."

"I had no idea that—"

"I'd enjoy looking at you? Running my hands over your magnificent body?"

"Thought that was just a guy thing."

"Nope. But now that you mention it..." She pulled her top over her head and let it drop to the floor. "Your turn."

He sucked in a breath. All that bounty. He started forward.

"Hang on." Pushing down her pants, she wiggled her hips. The pants slid to the floor and she stepped out of them. "Now we match."

His brain checked out. Her hip wiggle and the corresponding shimmy of her breasts had activated a primitive, single-minded drive. Reaching her in one stride, he wrapped her in a tight embrace. *Ahh.* He groaned as her plump breasts yielded to his pecs and her hips cradled his cock.

She pulled his head down, her mouth seeking his. Thrusting his tongue deep, he filled his hands with her tight little ass. Then he lifted her from the floor and edged closer to the side of the bed.

She whimpered and wrapped her legs around her hips. Perfect. Leaning over, he laid her on the bed and followed her down. Half-crazed and panting with anticipation, he broke away from her kiss and freed his hips. This would go fast.

Sliding from the bed, he stood and grabbed a packet from the nightstand.

"Hurry."

"I will." Her breathy plea fired him up even more. But he had the shakes, which slowed him down and he muttered a swear word.

"Jake?"

"It's fine." He rolled the condom in place. "Everything's fine." He glanced at the bed.

She'd scooted closer to the far edge to give him room. They'd make love crossways on the bed. Didn't matter on a king.

Nothing mattered but returning to Millie. Her luminescent gaze followed his progress as he put a knee on the bed. He kept eye contact as he made his way back to her smiling mouth, moist from his kisses.

Bracing his forearms on either side of her head, he eased down until the quivering tips of her breasts tickled his chest hair. "Hope I'm not dreaming this."

She traced the outline of his mouth with the tip of her finger. "Me, too. This is it, huh? The big moment?"

"Almost. Want to do something first." Dipping his head, he created a moist path over her silken skin until he reached her wine-dark nipple. Slowly he drew it into his mouth. His cock jerked as he cradled the weight of her breast and began to suck. Moaning, she cupped his head and arched into his caress.

His control was slipping, but what a way to go.

Hers was, too. Her fingertips pressed into his scalp and she began to pant. "Jake."

Okay, then. Releasing her breast, he eased up until they were face-to-face. His heart thundered and his ears buzzed. Soon. "You called?"

"I did." She found a new place to press with her strong fingers. Getting a firm hold on his glutes, she squeezed. "Now, please."

"Yes, ma'am." He moved into position. Paradise, it turned out, was easy to find and even easier to enter. She threw open the gates and he plunged right in.

Gasping, he bowed his head and stayed still while he struggled to master his response.

"Didja like that?"

He glanced up. "Uh-huh. You?"

She swallowed. "Very much." Her core muscles contracted.

He gasped again. "Oh, boy."

"Yeah. I'm..."

"Then here we go. Hang on, Millie." He began to stroke. Within seconds she climaxed and took him with her into the heart of the fire. Her cries blended with his deep groan as he buried his cock deep in her quivering channel.

His vision blurred. His pulse was whacked, racing at a speed that robbed him of breath. His world tilted, then gradually righted itself as the aftershocks tailed off.

Filling his chest with much needed air, he checked to see how she was doing. That dazed look in her green eyes probably mirrored his own. He stroked her flushed cheek. "We did it."

"Boy, howdy." Her voice was gravelly. She cleared her throat. "Is the top of my head still there?"

"Let's see." He laid his hand over her glossy copper hair. "Yes, ma'am. A little damp, but intact."

"All of me is damp. And you have little drops of sweat in your eyebrows."

He smoothed a finger over the right one. "So I do. I'd say something happened here."

"You're darn right. Millie and Jake finally got it on."

"Alert the media."

"Gonna post a big announcement online?"

He grinned. "Not tonight. Maybe tomorrow."

"You might as well. Everybody on this ranch knows what's happening here. No doubt the Babes do, too. With that many folks having inside info, we'll probably be a hot topic around the potbellied stove at the Apple Barrel."

"Do you care?"

"Not me. I wrangled Jake Lassiter into my bed. I'll be the envy of every bachelorette in town."

"And I'll be the envy of every unattached cowboy. But tonight, it's just you and me, kid." He feathered a kiss over her lips. "Tucked away in this cottage, shutting out the world."

A chime sounded from the floor.

"But not the texts." Millie glanced toward his jeans lying in a crumpled heap. "That's yours. Mine's in the kitchen."

"I'm ignoring it."

"What if the Brotherhood is having a cooking emergency?"

"Unlikely. I left them a huge pot of chili and baked them some cornbread."

"What if something's wrong in the barn?"

He gazed at her. "We're chock-a-block with wranglers on the Buckskin. They don't need me."

"But aren't you second in command after Matt? And he's—"

"Okay, okay." He eased away from her and left the bed. "I'll look at the text when I get back from the bathroom, but only because it came in after we'd had a most excellent time in your bed. Whoever it is caught me during a break."

Her laughter followed him down the hall. "Are we on a break?"

"Temporarily!" he called back. "Think of that as an appetizer."

"For the meal?"

"For the smorgasbord of lovemaking I have planned." *Smorgasbord.* She inspired him to come up with stuff like that. He was his best self when he was with Millie.

When he returned to the bedroom, she was gone and so was the lounge outfit and her slippers. "Millie?"

"In the living room," she called out. "Tending the fire. It almost died."

"By all means, let's keep the fires burning." He scooped up his briefs and jeans, still warm from his body heat. Not surprising. And when she'd wrapped her fingers around his....

He sucked in a breath. Better ditch that subject before he coaxed her back in here. He'd promised her dinner. He would deliver on that promise.

Cooking naked wasn't his thing, though. Grease spatters. After taking out his phone and laying it on the nightstand, he tugged on his underwear and his Wranglers. Might as well put on his shirt, too. He left the shirttails out, though. His version of loungewear.

At the last minute, he stuffed a condom in his jeans pocket. Just in case.

Grabbing the phone, he walked barefoot into the living room. The fire was crackling but she wasn't there. "Millie?"

"In the kitchen. Putting away what needs to be refrigerated."

Excellent point. He'd abandoned the groceries in favor of having hot sex with Millie. Good choice for him. Not so good for perishables.

He walked into the kitchen as she was bending over to put lettuce in the crisper at the bottom of the fridge. His fingers curled. She had a very inviting tush. His body reacted right on cue.

Straightening, she closed the door and turned. "Oh! I didn't hear you come in."

"No boots. Makes me stealthy."

She glanced at his bare feet. "There's something very arousing about seeing you in bare feet. Like you're ready for anything."

"I am."

Her gaze dropped to his fly and lifted to his face. Her eyes sparkled. "Is the break over?"

"Not unless you want it to be."

She smiled. "As I recall, you don't believe in missing meals."

"The steak and asparagus won't take long."

"And I've kept the fire going so we can eat in front of it."

"Right." He crossed to the counter where he'd left the steak marinating. "Let's get these under the broiler, and then—"

"Did you read your text?"

"I did not. Got distracted." He tapped his phone, checked the message and laughed.

"What?"

"Listen to this. It's from CJ. *Garrett likes to cook and he thinks the chili needs more chili pepper. He was polite about it, though. I informed him you made the chili and nobody was adding anything until I checked with you.*"

"Aw, that's so sweet. Told you the Brotherhood would miss your presence in the kitchen."

"Wait, there's more. *Hope you don't read this until three in the morning when you and Millie are limp as dish rags and buggy-eyed from hours of amazing sex.*"

She gave him an uneasy smile. "Three in the morning?"

"He's exaggerating." He stepped closer and slipped an arm around her waist. "We'll be fast asleep by two."

"I can't tell if you're kidding or not."

"I'm kidding."

She rested her palms on his chest. "It never occurred to me I might have trouble keeping up with you."

"This isn't an athletic event. I don't expect you to—"

"But you're in terrific shape. For all I know you could go until three in the morning. All night, maybe."

He smiled. "I might *want* to, because it feels so good, but that would be crazy. We work hard during the day. What sort of selfish jerk would wear you out so you dragged through the next day? Why would I want that for myself?"

"Then the smorgasbord you mentioned won't last for hours?"

"No."

She let out a sigh. "That's a relief. I think I know you so well, and yet I have no idea what you expect from a sexual relationship."

"I have no expectations."

"Really?"

"How could I? This is all new territory."

"But you've spent the night with women in the past."

"Not under these conditions. My underwear's in your dresser drawer. My shaving kit's in your bathroom. I came over loaded with groceries. And condoms. Probably way more than we'll need but I didn't know how many would be enough. I've never been in this situation before."

She met his gaze. "Neither have I."

"You haven't? I thought for sure you—"

"Just for a weekend. I've never spent a whole week with a guy, let alone moved in with someone long-term. Making room for your clothes felt… unsettling. Exciting, but still an adjustment."

"Huh. That shines a new light on things." He surveyed the counters, which had been neat when he arrived. Not so much, now. "I don't usually make a mess in the kitchen."

"It's not a mess. Only disorganized. And so what?" Her eyes twinkled. "We've been busy."

"Yep, and if I don't let go of you, we're liable to get busy again." He released her and backed away.

"Are you going to text CJ?"

"Thanks for reminding me." He typed a quick reply and tucked his phone away.

"What did you tell him?"

"To let Garrett add more chili pepper." He took the broiling pan out of the oven.

"Really? But you've been making it for years and the guys love your cooking."

"I know, but I had other things on my mind today. I could have gone a little lean on the chili pepper." He transferred the steaks to the pan and slid it under the broiler. "The guy honors his taste buds. That's gutsy in a new situation. If he wants to do some of the cooking, fine with me."

"Just not Friday night with chuck-wagon stew."

"Why not? Unlike Ezra, he'll follow my recipe. The Brotherhood will insist on it. And I won't be there this Friday night." He hesitated.

"Unless you've kicked me out by then." His gut tightened.

She moved into his space, then into his arms. "Why would I kick you out? You just gave me the most amazing climax of my life."

He gathered her close. "Yeah? You're not making that up?"

"Listen to me, Jake." She cupped his face in both hands. "During this week we're together, I might be short-tempered at times. I might get distracted and not respond the way you'd like. But I will never, ever lie to you."

He gazed into her eyes. "The most amazing climax of your life?"

"Yes." She smiled. "Totally worth the wait."

He kissed her. Couldn't help it. Not a kiss of seduction that would end in the bedroom. A kiss of gratitude.

He drew back from it eventually because he had something to say. "I'm a kidder. We both know that. But I won't lie to you. Not ever." He gazed into her smiling eyes. "Count on it."

_19_

Champagne, candlelight, a juicy steak dinner cooked by a handsome cowboy, a fire on the hearth and hot glances from the cook. What more could a girl want? Well, apple pie for dessert would be nice, and it was currently warming in the oven.

"Delicious meal, Jake." Millie lifted her champagne glass and saluted him. "Here's to your talents in the kitchen." Champagne loosened her tongue. "Matched only by your talents in the bedroom."

"Keep up that kind of talk and we'll have to skip the apple pie."

"I'm not skipping it. It smells heavenly."

"Then I'll bring it in." He stood and picked up the plates. "How about sitting on the couch for dessert?"

"Good idea. I'll add a couple more logs." Tending the fire was the only chore she'd had since he'd arrived. He'd insisted on fixing all the food and serving it, too. He'd even mentioned handling cleanup.

That was fine this first night when he clearly wanted to pamper her, but they needed to discuss a division of labor. Not a romantic topic, though, and romance was on the dinner menu, too. She'd let it go for now.

Once the fire was crackling again, she replaced the screen. "Need any help in there?"

"No, ma'am." He walked in with a bowl in each hand. "I decided on bowls and spoons. Seemed safer with dripping ice cream."

"Smart." She took a seat, choosing a spot near the middle of the roomy couch.

He handed her a bowl. "I don't think I've ever sat here." He settled down next to her, his hip and thigh nestled against hers.

"You must have. Think of all those times you and the guys have come over."

"We were mostly in the kitchen."

"But sometimes out here. Like when we roasted marshmallows that time."

"Seemed like the couch was for you and Kate. I might've taken that rocker over there, but I think I usually brought a chair from the kitchen."

"That rings a bell. Then you'd turn it around and straddle it." She scooped up a spoonful of warm pie and rapidly melting ice cream. "Why do guys do that?"

He paused, a dripping spoonful halfway to his mouth. "It looks manly. And gives us a chance to air out our boys."

"And show them off?"

He laughed. "Could be." He took another spoonful.

"That's my theory." As she continued to eat, she checked his position on the couch. "Even when they're not straddling a chair, guys feel the need to spread out."

Lifting his bowl away, he glanced down. "Sure enough." He flashed her a grin. "And you've noticed, so it must be an effective strategy."

She rolled her eyes. "Not really. I like a subtle approach."

"Good to know. I'll keep it in mind." He spooned up more pie and ice cream. "I love this combo."

"It's delicious." She took another bite. "Thanks for bringing it."

"My pleasure." He pointed his spoon at the bowl. "I like to heat up the pie until the filling is oozing out of the crust, then add ice cream that's hard as a rock."

She smiled. "Is this you being subtle?"

"Heck, no. I'm telling you how to create the perfect pie a la mode. Use soft ice cream and you're done before you even get started."

"Uh-huh."

"But now we get to this stage, where the crunchy parts are gone, leaving a creamy blend of juices that beg to be lapped up." Holding her gaze, he dipped the spoon into the bowl. "That's when I slow down, make every mouthful count."

Moisture gathered between her thighs. "I know what you're doing."

"Is it working?" Keeping the bowl under the dripping spoonful, he turned and offered it to her.

"Maybe." She let him feed her. The gentle slide of the spoon into her mouth was erotic as hell.

He drew it slowly back out and waited for her to swallow. Then he leaned over and kissed her with light easy pressure, a kiss that tasted of apple pie, ice cream and desire.

He nibbled on her lips, eased away, came back and teased her with more soft kisses. "It's working," he murmured as he took her bowl and set it, along with his, on the coffee table. "I'll stoke up the fire."

"You just did.

He laughed. "The other one." He stood and walked over to the hearth.

Evidently they were staying here. He had mentioned a smorgasbord, after all. "Anything I can do?"

"Don't think so." He set two more logs on the fire, surveyed the results and replaced the fire screen. Turning around, he sucked in a breath. "Except that."

"I thought you might like the idea." She folded her top and put it on the coffee table where she'd laid her folded pants. Stretching out on the couch, she propped a throw pillow behind her head.

"I love the idea." He unbuttoned his shirt as he walked toward her. "Firelight looks great on you."

Her body tightened in anticipation. "Can't wait to see you wearing it."

Stripping off his shirt, he laid it on the arm of the couch. Then he reached in his pocket.

"You had this in mind all along."

"Not all along." Leaning down, he laid the condom packet on the coffee table. "I'm a spontaneous kind of guy."

"Who tucks a condom in his pocket?"

He smiled. "Doesn't take up much room. Might come in handy. Scoot over a bit."

She made room for him and the denim material of his Wranglers pressed against her hip. "Aren't you missing a step, cowboy?"

"No, ma'am." He picked up a bowl of the now soupy dessert. "Thought you could help me finish this before I take off my jeans."

"You're kidding."

"Totally serious." He scooped up a spoonful of melted ice cream... and dribbled it over her breasts.

"Jake!"

"Whoops. Don't move or it'll run all over." He continued the process down the valley between her ribs and across her stomach.

"I can't believe you just did that."

"I'll take care of it. Just lie quietly and relax." Putting down the bowl, he lowered his head. With easy swipes of his warm tongue, he lapped at the creamy mixture. He took his time, pausing to suck gently on each nipple before moving on.

His lazy caresses heated her skin, stole her breath, tightened her core. Her thighs trembled. "FYI, this is not relaxing."

"No?" His breath tickled her moist skin as he continued his unhurried path down her body. "I'm shocked."

"You're not, either. You pinned me down with runny ice cream so I can't move while you—"

"Have my way with you?" He licked a path over her stomach. "Is it getting you hot?"

"Yes." Urgent need gripped her. "And you'd better be planning to—"

"I am." He dipped his tongue into her navel. "Done."

She started to sit up.

"Wait a sec." He slid one arm under her shoulders and the other under her knees. "One more thing."

"A change of venue?"

"Not yet." Instead of picking her up, he repositioned her so she was sitting on the couch with her feet on the floor. "I haven't finished my dessert."

"Stay away from that bowl, cowboy. I've had enough of—"

"Not touching the bowl." He knelt at her feet, fire in his eyes. "My dessert is you." With calm intent, he hooked her knees over his shoulders, slid his hands under her bottom and kissed his way along her quivering inner thigh.

She was undone, dazzled by his bold move. Trembling with anticipation, she waited…

At last his tongue made contact. The jolt of pleasure shot through her, a live wire igniting sparks in every part of her eager body. With a cry of surrender, she abandoned herself to wonder, to delight, to Jake.

He gave her a climax, then another, leaving her limp and gulping for air. Cradling her in his arms, he carried her closer to the fire and laid her gently on the braided rug. A zipper buzzed, foil crackled and he moved over her, murmuring in his low, sexy voice as he slipped effortlessly into her drenched channel.

He coaxed her to another climax before claiming his own. Gasping her name, he thrust deep. She held on tight, absorbing the tremors rolling through his muscular body.

Gradually his breathing slowed. She drifted in a hazy world of warmth and comfort until a cool breeze wafted over her damp skin as he left. Soft material blocked the chill.

Safe. Happy. Strong arms carried her to bed. She slept.

Sometime during the night, she woke, disoriented when she touched a warm, solid body lying next to her. "What the—"

"It's me." He wrapped her in his arms. "Jake."

"Oh." She sighed and nestled into the shelter of his embrace. The hard length of his cock pressed against her thigh. With astonishing speed, the embers of desire flared to life. "Again, please."

"You're sure?"

"I'm sure."

He made slow, easy love to her until they both came. Then he slipped out of bed to dispose of the condom.

When he returned, she stroked his bristly cheek. "Thank you."

His chuckle was low and intimate. "Don't mention it." Gathering her close, he fell asleep quickly.

But she lay awake, marveling that she was sharing her bed, at long last, with Jake. If he had misgivings, he'd clearly shoved them aside to give her an amazing night of lovemaking. He seemed at ease with her and his surroundings.

It probably helped that he was familiar with the house. He liked her dream bed, too. That was a very good sign. Gradually, sleep claimed her.

When she awoke, Jake was gone, the bedroom door was closed and water was running in the kitchen. She glanced at the digital clock on the nightstand. Ten after four. Even if Jake had barn duty, he wouldn't have to get up until five or so.

Climbing out of bed, she went to her closet and pulled out her white terry robe with the Buckskin Ranch logo. She had to move his shirts to get to it. Made her smile to have them there. She put on the robe and tied the sash.

Crazy guy. Dollars to donuts he was doing last night's dishes because he'd made love to her instead of cleaning up the kitchen as promised. Touching, but totally unnecessary. They needed to talk.

20

Jake made a policy of keeping his word and he'd promised to clean up after the meal. Then he'd left the kitchen a mess. Wasn't his style, and besides, caked-on food was tougher to wash off. Wanting Millie with the heat of a thousand suns was no excuse. He should've planned better.

The image of dirty dishes and pans had prodded him awake about twenty minutes ago. He'd listened to Millie breathe, trying to gauge whether he'd wake her if he got up. Likely not. Great sex made for deep sleep. Unless something had been left unfinished.

If he'd taken time out to do the dishes last night, though, their sexy vibe would have been impacted. She might have insisted on helping and he'd wanted to handle the dinner and dishes on their first night together.

So here he was, making up for lost time. He'd closed both the bedroom door and the kitchen door for extra insurance that Millie wouldn't be able to hear him working. He'd bypassed the dishwasher in favor of a sink of hot sudsy water. Dishwashers were noisy and chances were good Millie was attuned to the sound of one operating on her own turf.

When the kitchen door opened, he turned from the sink. "Damn, I'm sorry, Millie. I tried to be quiet."

"You were." She padded over in her bare feet, looking cute as the dickens in that big fluffy robe. "You didn't wake me. But when I realized you weren't in bed and I heard the water running in here, I figured out what you were up to."

He grabbed a towel. "Handling what I left undone last night." Drying his hands, he flipped the towel over his shoulder and drew her close. "Morning, pretty lady." He kissed her carefully, mindful of his beard. "I'll do a better job of that after I've shaved."

She smiled up at him. "Morning, Jake. Why didn't you use the dishwasher?"

"It's noisy."

Her expression softened. "And might wake me up?"

"Yes, ma'am."

"That's very sweet." She glanced at the dish strainer. "Looks like you're about done."

"Just the broiler pan left. Do you want coffee? I could make—"

"I'll put on the coffee." She slipped out of his arms and grabbed the empty carafe from the coffeemaker on the counter.

Seemed as if she wanted the job, so he didn't argue. "Okay. That'd be great."

She had to maneuver around all the clean dishes in the strainer but she managed to fill the carafe with water. "Then I'll dry these while you scrub the pan."

"No, ma'am. The dishes are my job and I skipped it last—"

"Because you were making love to me, as I recall." She poured the water in the coffeemaker.

"That's no excuse."

"It's the best excuse in the world." She pushed the button on the electric coffee grinder.

There was no talking over that noise, so he waited until she dumped the coffee in the basket and turned on the pot.

"The thing is, I should have planned better."

"How?" She pulled a clean dishtowel from a drawer and picked up a plate from the strainer. "Unless you have superpowers, you can't be in two places at once."

"No, but I'm sure there's a solution. I just didn't think of it." He returned to the sink where the broiler pan was soaking. If she was determined to dry the dishes, he wouldn't argue with her about it. He didn't want to argue about *anything.*

She moved with brisk efficiency emptying the strainer and putting everything away. "In the meantime, let's figure out a distribution of labor."

"For what?" He scrubbed the remnants of the steak from the broiler pan.

"Everything." She leaned against the counter, the dishtowel in one hand, waiting for him to finish with the pan. "Last night it sounded as if you'd like to do most of the cooking."

"I would. And the cleanup."

"You take on both things in the bunkhouse?"

"No. The guys rotate with cleanup, but—"

"How about letting me handle cleanup, then?"

He frowned. "When I get inspired, I dirty up a lot of pans."

"So what?"

"I don't like the idea of giving you more work." He bore down and the last bit of dried steak came off.

"Do you feel that way about the Brotherhood cleaning up after you?"

"There's more of them. The job's spread out." He rinsed the pan and put it in the strainer. "If you'll give me the towel, I'll get this."

"My job." She flashed him a quick smile. "You may not believe me, but I enjoy kitchen cleanup."

"You won't say that after I've done some creative cooking. The guys complain all the time about the number of pots and pans. Last night was straightforward. If I'd at least put everything to soak, it would have been a snap."

"Then how about this? Before we start fooling around, we put the dishes in the sink with some soapy water and leave 'em for me to do in the morning."

"Or I could get up early and—"

"No, doggone it! That's what I'm trying to avoid."

His gut clenched. "Then, sure. We can do that."

"Jake?" She put down the broiler pan and the towel and came toward him. "Are you okay?"

"I'm fine."

"You didn't look fine a second ago. You looked stressed."

He took a deep breath. "I'm fine. Listen, I'd better go grab a shower." He glanced at the kitchen clock. "I should have enough time to make us breakfast."

"I could start something while you're in the shower." She peered at him, her eyes filled with uncertainty.

"That's okay. I'll be quick." He left the kitchen. A hot shower would calm him down. Millie hadn't been angry, just irritated. He'd certainly irritated her before. Angered her before, too.

But nothing had been on the line. Now everything was on the line. And he was jumpy as hell.

Closing the bathroom door, he stripped off his clothes and turned on the shower. Two bath towels, one green and one blue, hung beside the stall. Which was he supposed to use?

He shut off the water. Her eyes were green and his were blue. But that didn't mean she'd assign towels that way. He took the blue one and wrapped it around his waist before walking back to the kitchen.

She sat at the table with a cup of coffee. He caught her staring into space. Startled her, too.

She took a quick breath. "Problem?"

"Didn't know which towel to use."

"Oh! All the towels are clean, so it doesn't matter. I would have used whichever one you didn't."

"I grabbed this one."

"Good choice. Matches your eyes." She gave him a once-over and smiled. "Better get out of here before I jump your bones."

"I won't be long." He headed back down the hall. She'd have extra laundry because of him. She and Kate must have a system for laundry, same as the Brotherhood. He'd ask.

Draping the towel over the rack, he turned on the water again. The shower was sparkling clean. He'd pitch in to keep it that way. Because of his job, he'd be tracking more dirt into the house than she or Kate normally did. He put vacuuming on the list. They hadn't discussed any of that. They'd just hopped into bed.

He stepped under the hot spray. Hell, he hadn't thought about shampoo, either. The Brotherhood bought one giant bottle of whatever was on sale and shared it.

She had some, so he used it. Smelled flowery, like her. Her soap did, too. He didn't mind, but he might hear about it from Rafe when he arrived at the barn.

Unless he planned to buy his own soap and shampoo, he needed to take note of her brand and buy her some to replace what he used. What else was he forgetting?

Firewood. She might not make a fire every night during her normal routine. The Brotherhood took care of cutting firewood for themselves, Henri and this cottage. He'd check the woodpile later today in case it needed replenishing.

He didn't allow himself much time in the shower and he made fast work of his shaving routine, too. Uh-oh, no clean clothes to put on. Should he wear a towel the short distance to Millie's room? Nah.

Tidying up the bathroom, he picked up his clothes and walked quickly down the hall. When he stepped through the bedroom door, she was in there making the bed. He couldn't offer to help unless he wanted to be her naked assistant. Not cool.

She paused and grinned at him. "Must be my lucky day."

"Didn't think to take my clean clothes in with me."

"Please don't apologize."

"I'm not on my game yet." He put his pile of clothes on the dresser and opened the drawer where he'd stashed his briefs and T-shirts.

"Your game looks good from here. Wish we had time to play."

"So do I." He pulled on his briefs. "My buddy's very interested in the idea." He tugged a clean T-shirt over his head and turned around.

"I can see that." She crossed her arms. "Please give me points for not coming over there."

"Only if you'll give me points for staying put."

"Points given. I need to get out of here. What if I prep some things for breakfast?"

"Sure." He walked to the closet and took one of his shirts off a hanger. "Might as well pour the juice and get out the bacon and eggs. And the cinnamon rolls."

"Fried or scrambled?"

"Scrambled is faster." He shoved his arms into the sleeves. "You can crack half-a-dozen eggs into a bowl if you want."

"Will do." Her gaze swept over him again. "It's been fun watching you get dressed, but it's more exciting in reverse." She took a deep breath. "Okay, I'm outta here." She turned and hurried through the door.

21

Jake cooked up a delicious breakfast. Too bad they had to rush through it. Or maybe not. Millie wasn't ready to tackle the subject of shared duties again this morning. She scored a small victory when Jake left the dishes in sudsy water in the sink.

She walked him to the door and he gathered her close. "Rubs me the wrong way to leave those dishes."

"I'll make it up to you." She nestled against him. "Next time I get a chance, I'll rub you the right way."

He groaned. "Wish to hell I hadn't agreed to drive into Great Falls today or I could stop by during my lunch break."

She'd suggest asking someone else to go, but she'd be wasting her breath. When he said he'd do something it was cast in stone. "The time will go fast."

"Not fast enough to suit me." He gazed into her eyes. "I'm gonna kiss you one time and then vamoose. If I leave in a hurry, it's because staying means a second kiss, and a third, and—"

"Next thing you know, you'll be late for work."

"Exactly." He lowered his head. "I'll miss you."

"I'll miss you, too." When his mouth found hers, her world fell into place. Whatever speed bumps lay ahead, the physical bond between them was perfect. Each kiss was new, yet as familiar as if she'd spent years making love to him.

He deepened the kiss and untied the sash of her robe.

She didn't stop him. Didn't need to. His sense of duty was stronger than she'd given him credit for. He smoothed his hands over her curves, starting with her hips and ending by cradling her breasts and squeezing gently.

She moaned and sucked on his tongue. He might have a sense of duty second to none, but hers was wavering.

His breathing roughened. But instead of pushing her robe off her shoulders, he slowly released his hold and lifted his head. "Time to go. Or I never will."

She nodded as he pulled the lapels of her robe together and tied the sash.

"See you tonight." He grabbed his hat from a small table by the door and put it on. Touching two fingers to the brim, he opened the door and stepped through it into the semi-darkness of the coming dawn. Moments later his truck roared to life and he drove away.

In less than twenty-four hours she'd learned more about Jake than she had in all the years they'd worked together. He had prodigious strengths and touching weaknesses. This experiment would be a challenge, but she welcomed it more than ever.

She was showered, dressed and about to clean up the kitchen when Kate messaged her. *I texted Rafe, so I know Jake's at the barn. I left my favorite earrings there. Can I pop over before I head to the dining hall?*

Sure. Have time for coffee?

Half a cup.

Kate's *half-a-cup* routine was familiar. She didn't mean it. She had about thirty minutes before she had to start cooking breakfast for the guests. Plenty of time for coffee and conversation.

Her forgotten earrings might be an excuse to stop by. Millie didn't care. She could use some girl talk.

She poured two cups of coffee, opened the box of cinnamon rolls and took a couple of dessert plates out of the cupboard.

The front door opened. "Fe-fi-fo-fum, I smell the sweat of a sexy man!"

"You do not," Millie called from the kitchen. "He showered this morning and he used my soap and shampoo so he smells just like me."

"I doubt it." She walked into the kitchen, her short curly hair still damp from the shower. "He has way too much testosterone to be overpowered by your girly shampoo and soap." She glanced at the cinnamon rolls. "Ooo, what do we have here?"

"He got these for breakfast. He brought so much food, Kate. And last night's meal was—"

"Don't care, don't care, don't care. Tell me about the sex."

Millie laughed. "No."

"Okay then, was it spectacular?"

"Yes."

"That's it? *Yes*?"

Millie laughed. "If you're fishing for details, you won't get them. All I'll say is that he made me very, very happy."

"I'm pea-green with envy." She sat down and helped herself to a cinnamon roll.

"I thought you'd sworn off men." Millie joined her at the table and put a cinnamon roll on her plate.

"I have no desire to cohabit with one, but if I could get the goodies without the angst, that would be awesome."

"Good luck with that."

Kate put down her cinnamon roll and gazed across the table. "You have angst already?"

"Nothing major. Not yet."

"That sounds ominous. What happened?"

"Early this morning, *very* early, we got into a discussion-slash-argument because he doesn't want me doing the dishes, and I—"

"Wait. You were arguing for your right to wash dishes? What's wrong with you?"

"It's complicated."

"No, it's not. Let him wash the freaking dishes while you eat bonbons and watch TV. Most women would kill for that setup."

"I suppose it sounds crazy, but... anyway, that's not the issue. We worked it out. I got him to leave the breakfast dishes in the sink."

Kate sighed and shook her head. "Evidently great sex has altered your brain chemistry."

Millie smiled. ""It was important because... never mind. The bottom line is that I got frustrated and raised my voice a little. And he quietly freaked out."

"He did?" She looked confused. "Are you sure that was the reason?"

"Pretty sure."

"But you've raised your voice to him dozens of times. I've only been here eighteen months, and even I know that. Was it more like yelling?"

"Absolutely not. Just more forceful than my normal speech. He abruptly caved and looked like he'd seen a ghost."

"Hm." Kate sipped her coffee. "Maybe he did. The ghost of his parents' awful relationship."

"But he said they had screaming fights where they threw things at each other. This was just normal give and take."

"I believe you. But instead of being in the bunkhouse during one of our get-togethers, or at the Moose on Saturday night, you were alone in this cozy domestic setting. Maybe that amplified it for him."

Millie groaned. "God, I hope not. Walking on eggshells isn't going to work for me. If we're going to live together for a week, we have details to work out."

"Like what? Who brings the can of whipped cream?"

"Be serious."

"Just trying to lighten the mood." She took another sip of her coffee. "I'm with you on the eggshells thing. You won't be on the same page all the time. Then you either compromise or agree to disagree and move on."

"Which he *can*. He does it all the time with the guys."

"And in a sense, you used to be one of the guys. Now you're not."

"And I'm thrilled about that. I was sick to death of being buddies and nothing more. He's the one, Kate. He always has been."

"Then you have to go all in."

"I think I'm already there." She met Kate's gaze. "Heaven help me."

"You can add my support to whatever you get from heaven."

"Thanks, Kate."

"Not that I'm any great shakes at this. I've tried and failed. I can tell you for sure what doesn't work, though."

"What's that?"

"Avoiding the issues. Thinking a good roll in the hay means that you've solved them. It doesn't. They'll come back to bite you in the ass."

22

Jake had caught his share of ribbing from Rafe about how sweet he smelled. Then CJ had showed up and piled on. Those two had been relentless.

Originally he'd planned to pick up a small bottle of something less floral while he was running errands in Great Falls. He'd get just enough for the week at Millie's.

But after the guys made such a big deal out of it, he got his back up. He searched for and found her exact brand and bought several bottles of it. The conditioner, too. He'd never bothered with it before but maybe he'd start. Her hair certainly was silky to the touch.

All of her was silky. He tossed the bag of shampoo and conditioner in the passenger seat and turned the truck toward home. *Home.* Where Millie of the incredibly soft skin would be waiting for him.

Their goodbye kiss had been damned hot. It was a wonder he'd made it out the door. Less than an hour and he'd be kissing her hello. Would she have on that same outfit with nothing underneath? Or one like it?

Well, why not? It was just the two of them. Why would she bother with underwear? He should have taken a pair of sweats over to her house so he could do basically the same thing.

Yeah, if they both wore easy-off clothes, that would make sense. Then they—

A siren wailed. Sheesh, the cop was right on his tail, lights flashing. Must have come up fast. Nobody was in the other lane. Why didn't he just go around?

Because he's after you, idiot. A glance at the speedometer told him why. Damn, and double damn. He turned on his flashers and pulled to the side of the road. He hadn't had a ticket in *years.*

That wasn't the most embarrassing part, though. He'd texted Millie that he was on his way. No hiding this screw-up.

He shut off the engine and rolled down the window as the officer approached. Not a *he* but a *she.* More women were becoming troopers— it had been on the news—but he'd never encountered one, likely because he wasn't in the habit of driving twenty miles over the speed limit.

He rested his hands on the steering wheel as she approached.

"Good afternoon."

"Good afternoon, officer."

"Do you know why I pulled you over?"

"Yes, ma'am. I was speeding."

"Do you know how fast you were going?"

"Last I checked, about nineteen miles over." Sounded better than twenty.

"I clocked you at twenty-two over."

"Yes, ma'am. I was speeding. No question about that."

"And unaware of your surroundings."

"No, ma'am. I heard that siren immediately."

"What about the lights?"

"Saw those, too."

"Apparently not, since I've been following you with lights flashing for approximately a mile."

Yikes. "I see."

"Not very well, it seems. Prior to putting on my lights, I was behind you for a couple of miles. Usually when folks see the black and white, they slow down. You went faster."

"I allowed myself to be distracted."

"Cell phone?"

"No. It's in the console."

"I don't smell alcohol. Are you on any medications?"

"No, ma'am. Just eager to get home, is all."

Her expression softened. "Kids?"

"No, ma'am. My... girlfriend." The word didn't begin to describe Millie. It was too generic and nothing about her was generic.

"Ah." She nodded. "I need to see your license, registration and proof of insurance, please."

He fetched his documents from the console and handed them over.

She examined them and gave them back. "I'm going to issue a warning instead of a ticket, Mr. Lassiter. We don't have a designation for driving while in love. Please be more careful in the future."

"Yes, ma'am. Thank you, ma'am." *Driving while in love?* The phrase bounced around in his brain through the rest of the process until he finally bid the officer goodbye.

Taking the phone from the console, he texted Millie. *I've been delayed. Be there ASAP.* He tucked the phone back in the console, started the truck and checked for traffic before pulling out.

How to deal with the rest of the drive so he'd stay focused on the job at hand? He'd never encountered this problem. *Driving while in love.*

It wasn't love. Sex, yes. Love, no. That took longer to develop. That—he checked his speedometer and he was five miles over. Eased up on the pedal. Switched on the radio.

No good. They would have to be playing *Breathe.* He switched stations. More country love songs. Naturally. He switched again and got some dude dissecting the stock market. Perfect.

Except five minutes of that boring stuff and he was back to Millie, the woman he liked a lot but didn't love. That took months, years. She might think she loved him, though, and that could cause—whoops, five miles over.

Since the radio was no help, he turned it off and started singing. He had a limited repertoire of songs he knew by heart and they were mostly from his kindergarten days. He barreled through

Old MacDonald Had a Farm, She'll Be Comin' 'Round the Mountain, and *There Was an Old Woman Who Swallowed a Fly*.

What else? Nothing. Had to start over with Old MacDonald. Damn, he was dying, here. Longest. Trip. Ever.

He turned down the ranch road with a sigh of relief. Couldn't speed on the ranch road. Shocks wouldn't take it. *Almost there.*

Except he had to drop off stuff at the barn before heading over to the cottage. The feed store in Great Falls was running a huge sale on hay nets, which had prompted the trip. The ones in the barn were raggedy. He'd also picked up a new wheelbarrow at a decent price and some replacement grooming supplies.

He backed the truck in near the barn door, climbed out and went around to lower the tailgate.

Nick came out. "Heard your truck. Let me give you a hand."

"Thanks. You're welcome to haul in the wheelbarrow box."

"You bet."

Jake had to smile. Nick preferred tasks that required muscle. The harder he worked his body, the more he could eat. And the guy loved to eat. "Picked up several packages of those chocolate sandwich cookies you asked for."

"Awesome!" Nick hefted the large box that contained the disassembled wheelbarrow. "Thanks, bro! Don't know why they don't carry those in the market."

Jake took the bags of grooming supplies. "Because nobody buys them but you. Folks here want fresh-baked stuff."

"I get that, but I like the way you can twist these apart and lick the frosting. You can't do that with bakery cookies."

"And how old are you?"

Nick grinned. "Old enough to know what I like and stick to it."

"I respect that. I promise not to tease you about those anymore. I'll look for a different topic."

"God, I hope so. I don't know what I'd do if you turned into a sober-sides."

"Not gonna happen." He let Nick go ahead of him into the barn since he had the heavier load.

"Glad to hear it. Guess I should stick this in the tack room until there's time to put it together."

"Yeah, I'll wait to sort out the grooming supplies, too." He followed Nick through the tack room door. "Tomorrow's good enough. I—hey there." He glanced over as the new hire walked in.

"Hey, Jake." Garrett was a tall guy. Easy smile. "That was damn good chili."

"Just needed a little more kick, I take it."

He shrugged. "Nobody thought so but me. I didn't goose it up much."

"It was good both ways," Nick said. "Putting in more chili pepper meant drinking more hard cider to cool my mouth down, but I don't have a problem with that."

Jake's curiosity got the better of him. "What's on the menu for tonight?" He'd left CJ with a list of ideas that were easy to fix and would make use of what was in the fridge and the pantry.

Garrett shoved back his hat. "I picked up some chicken breasts today at the market. I've got them marinating."

Oh, did he, now? "Marinating in what?"

"Stuff you had on hand—olive oil, lemon juice, brown sugar, garlic, a few other things. Your spice drawer is impressive. Couldn't ask for better."

"Well, that's good, then." Evidently Garrett would handle a meal or two. The Brotherhood probably appreciated it. "CJ's a big help, I'm sure."

"He is. Awesome chopping skills. Very loyal, too. He wasn't about to let me add that pepper until he checked with you."

"We've fixed a lot of meals together."

"Speaking of that, I'd better head back to the bunkhouse and put the chicken in the oven. I just wanted to stop by and say what a great setup you've created."

"Thanks. Enjoy."

"I'm having a hell of a time." Garrett touched two fingers to the brim of his hat and left.

Nick glanced at Jake. "Don't worry. We won't let him take over. This is strictly because you're at Millie's."

"Yeah, but if the guy can cook, you'd get more variety if we switch off."

"We don't need more variety. We like the things you fix. They've become Brotherhood food traditions."

Jake gazed at him. "That's nice to hear. Listen, has anyone told Garrett about the Brotherhood?"

"Not yet. Leo asked Henri if she'd mentioned it and she hasn't. Thought it was ours to reveal."

"But how? And do we let him in?"

"While he was at the market getting the chicken today, some of us had a chance to talk about it. We decided not to bring it up this week with Matt on his honeymoon and you at Millie's."

"We should have talked about this sooner. Henri told us she'd hire someone to replace Seth. We should've had a game plan."

"I know." Nick sighed.

"We work as a team. I don't see how we can have our exclusive group and leave him completely out of it."

"On the other hand, we can't just say presto-change-o, you're in."

"No. Especially not until he's been here awhile and we get to know him. Find out if he's worthy."

"Exactly." Nick resettled his hat. "We need to see what he's made of. That'll take a while."

Jake nodded. "We can talk it over with Matt when he gets home. I've forgotten when he and Lucy are due back."

"Late Thursday night. But in the meantime, we can all be thinking about how we want to handle it."

"Definitely. I'll start making notes on my phone."

Nick chuckled. "Yeah, sure you will."

"Hey. I will."

"Nah, don't worry about it, lover boy. Those of us who aren't playing house will work on it." He tugged his hat lower. "Let's get those hay nets and cookies out of your truck so you can get your butt over to Miss Millie's place."

At the mention of her name, Jake's focus made a one-eighty. "Yeah, let's do that." Too bad he hadn't put some chicken breasts in a marinade before he'd left this morning. Could be a good plan for tomorrow night's dinner, though.

<u>23</u>

When Jake's truck pulled in, Millie went out to greet him. Didn't stop for a jacket. She couldn't have stayed inside if someone had glued her boots to the floor.

By the time he'd shut off the motor and opened his door, she was there, climbing up to the running board, reaching for him. "I thought you'd *never* get here."

"Long trip." Swinging around in the seat, he spread his knees and pulled her in close. With a groan, his mouth came down on hers.

She wrapped her arms around his neck and wedged herself in tighter. Leaning into his kiss, she slackened her jaw and invited him to go deeper.

His grip tightened and he lifted his head only long enough to gasp out her name. Then he plunged his tongue into her mouth again, his breathing ragged. She squirmed in his arms, desperate to get closer, to press her aching body against his.

Wrenching his mouth away, he dragged in air. "This is crazy. We can't... do this here."

"I just had to—"

"Yeah." His chest heaved. "Me, too." He gazed into her eyes. "Damn, Millie."

She swallowed. "Think we can... make it inside?"

"Have to." He cleared the hoarseness from his throat. "Not having sex in your front yard."

She eased away from him. "Let's make a run for it."

He nodded.

She climbed down, her balance shaky. He was beside her in two seconds, his strong arm circling her shoulders.

"Come on." He took off, leaving the truck door standing open as he propelled her across the small yard and up the porch steps.

In her haste, she'd left both the front door and the screen open. He flung the screen wider and nudged the door aside with his booted foot. Once they were both in, he kicked it closed.

Then he was kissing her again, his breathing harsh as he backed her against the door, scooped his hands under her hips and lifted her up. She wrapped her legs around his waist as he continued to ravish her mouth.

Bracing her against the door, he pulled her tight against his package and kissed his way to her throat. "Unbutton your shirt."

She slipped the buttons free with trembling fingers. He followed her progress with his lips, tracing a path over her collarbone and down the slope of her breast. When she reached for the front clasp of her black lace bra, his low hum of approval sent moisture to her overheated lady parts.

Dipping his head, he circled her nipple with his tongue. "You're delicious." His throaty murmur and his warm breath on her skin made her shiver with excitement.

He nibbled gently, scraping his teeth lightly over her taut nipple before finally drawing it slowly into his mouth. His cheeks hollowed as he gradually took in more, creating a seductive tug that arrowed straight to her womb.

As he began to suck, he rocked forward, putting pressure on an exquisitely sensitive area. She gasped as her core clenched. He eased back and rocked forward again. And again. And again.

She came apart, arching away from the door as undulations from a powerful climax left her helplessly clinging to his broad shoulders and gulping for air. He held her in his firm grip, keeping the connection tight until her breathing gradually slowed.

Gradually releasing his hold on her breast, he raised his head. His hot glance traveled over her bare, quivering breasts. Then he met her gaze and gave her a smile of male satisfaction. "It's a start."

"You're..." She swallowed. "You're amazing."

"It's not me." His voice was thick with restraint. "It's you." Shifting his hold, he supported her back with one arm and her hips with the other as he headed for the bedroom, his breath coming fast. "I'm desperate, Millie."

"Tell me what you need."

"You. Now."

"I'm here." Heat flared again, tightening her body, preparing it for more of his intense loving.

Moving quickly, he laid her crossways on the bed. "This won't be elegant." He tugged off her boots. "If you could take off—"

"Done." She wiggled out of her jeans and panties as he tore off his jacket and grabbed a packet from the nightstand drawer.

Leaving on the rest of his clothes, he quickly unzipped his jeans, shoved down his briefs and rolled on the condom. Braced above her, his jeans pressed against her thighs and his shirt brushing her stomach, he slid his hands beneath her hips, probed once, and pushed home.

With fire in his eyes, he began to thrust, slowly at first, then faster, and faster yet. His jaw tightened. "Come for me. Come again, Millie. I love making you come."

As if she could help it. When he brought the heat, she melted. He bore down and she surrendered to the wonder she found in his arms. When he surrendered, too, his orgasm pulsing in rhythm with hers, she wrapped herself in the glory of the moment. Jake was home.

* * *

The light had faded from the sky, leaving the bedroom in darkness. Millie lay on her back, naked and gasping. Orgasm number three.

When Jake had recovered from the first round in this bed, he'd disposed of the condom and stripped off his clothes. She'd ditched her shirt and bra. They'd fooled around, exchanging teasing caresses and sexy talk until they'd worked themselves into a lather. And made love again.

Jake reached for her hand and laced his fingers through hers. "It's because I haven't seen you all day. If I hadn't gone to Great Falls, then—"

"We would have had a sexy lunch break?"

"The thought had occurred to me. But today it wasn't possible. Tomorrow, on the other hand…"

"What if it makes it tough to go back to work?"

"I'll take that risk." He squeezed her hand. "But I'm only speaking for myself."

"What about lunch? I'm not sure we have time for both eating and making love."

"PB and J. That takes no time at all."

"Wait." She propped herself on her elbow to look in his direction, even though he was in shadows. "I've heard you say PB and J is not a sufficient lunch."

"It's not if you eat it all the time, but—"

"You'll cut corners for great sex?"

"Damn straight." The mattress shifted as he rolled to his side, facing her. "Wouldn't you?"

"Yes, but I never thought I'd hear you say it."

"When I made that statement, I didn't have enough information."

"Meaning?"

"I hadn't made love to you. You're a game-changer."

"Thank you." Global statement, there. How did she change the game, exactly? Did she want to ask that question tonight when she was flushed and happy from three lovely orgasms? No.

She'd ask something easy, instead. "What delay did you run into this afternoon?"

He sighed. "Got pulled over."

"Why?"

"Speeding."

"But you don't speed."

"I did this time. It was a legitimate traffic stop. I was more than twenty miles over."

"Jake! That's not like you."

"It was today."

Something in his voice clued her in. "Was it me? You were rushing to get back because of me?"

"Yes, ma'am. But—"

"Oh, dear." She scooted closer and stroked his cheek. "Let me share the cost of the ticket."

"No ticket. She let me off with a warning."

Millie laughed. "Oh, she did, did she? What did you say?"

"That I was eager to get home. She asked about kids, and I said no, that I had a girlfriend."

His use of *home* touched her. "She must be a romantic. I'm glad you didn't get a ticket, but if you had, I would have shared the cost."

"No way."

"It's only fair. You were speeding because of me." A remarkable event. He was a steady driver. She'd ridden with him enough to know.

"My mistake, my responsibility." Underneath the casual statement lay a hint of steel.

But she had a point to make. "Speeding is out of character for you. If we hadn't set up this new arrangement and had sex last night, you wouldn't have had a lead foot on your way—"

"But I didn't get a ticket, so it doesn't matter."

"But you could have if a different trooper had come along. And I would feel partially respons—"

"Nope, doesn't work that way." He released her hand and sat up.

She sat up, too. "I only think that—"

"I know what you think. I disagree. I need to start dinner." He left the bed, pulled on his clothes and walked out of the room.

Great. Twenty-four hours into the experiment and they had another issue. But they had plenty of time before the workday would separate them again.

She wouldn't look for sex to solve the problem, though. She was with Kate on that. A roll in the hay wasn't the answer.

24

Jake took the pork chops, a few small potatoes and an onion out of the fridge. His heart wasn't in it, but this was what he'd planned for dinner, so might as well fix the meal.

And so it began. He'd allowed himself to get irritated with Millie and then he'd stomped out of the room. Before long he'd be yelling at her the way his father had yelled at his mother.

After buttoning his shirt, he sliced the potatoes and onions, set two heavy frying pans on the stove, put a chunk of butter in each and turned on the heat.

Why couldn't Millie understand that his driving behavior was his business? He'd made the mistake, not her. If he couldn't concentrate because he was focused on making love to her, that was his problem.

The pork chops were sizzling and the country-style potatoes and onion were sautéing when she walked in wearing the fluffy white robe that looked innocent and was sexier than hell.

"Smells great." Her smile was a little off-center.

He gave her credit for smiling at all. She was terrific that way, a bright spirit shining light on everyone around her.

He checked the food on the stove and turned to her. "I'm sorry. I shouldn't have left so abruptly."

"I understand. I bruised your ego."

"You bruised my—no! This isn't about my ego."

"Sure it is."

"Millie, it's not. It's about me taking responsibility for my actions."

She gazed at him. "Actions that are impacted by my actions. We're in this together, at least I'd like to think we are. Unless you're determined to be the Lone Ranger."

His stomach pitched. "I don't want to be."

"Good, because we've shared some intense body contact, buster, the kind that leaves a major impression on a person's psyche. Maybe you can shove that to the back of your mind, but I can't."

He took a deep breath. "I can't, either."

"At least we're on the same page regarding the sexy times." The topic seemed to stick in her throat. She cleared it. "But living together for a week, or a week minus a day, to be precise, requires sharing the load in other areas besides the bedroom."

He exhaled. "If that means agreeing that we should split my non-existent traffic ticket, then I'm—"

"Since that's a touchy subject, let's ignore it for now."

"Hallelujah." He turned back to the stove, flipped over the pork chops and stirred the potatoes.

"But we need to address some other items that go along with sharing a living space. We haven't talked about laundry."

"I don't want to add to your workload. At the end of the week, I'll take my towel and washcloth back to the bunkhouse to be washed and returned."

"And that is *exactly* what I'm talking about. What did you do with your clothes from yesterday? They weren't on top of the dresser when I went back in the room later."

"I'm having them framed." He ducked his head so she wouldn't see his grin.

"Jake."

He kept his back to her and shrugged. "I'm a sentimental guy. Last night was special. It was either bronzed or framed, and framed is cheaper."

A tiny snort of laughter. Good sign.

He laid it on thicker. "It'll look really cool when it's done. I thought about asking for your green lounge outfit to add in there, but I was hoping you might wear it again sometime this week so I ditched that idea."

"Clearly you don't want to talk about laundry."

"I do not. The chops and potatoes are almost done. If you'd be willing to get out the salad fixings, I'll put that together."

"How about letting me put it together?"

He'd rather have her make the salad than do his laundry, which is where that convo was likely headed. "That would be great."

She rummaged in the refrigerator. "So about this traffic stop."

"Millie."

"I won't bring up the touchy part. I'm just curious how it went. I haven't been pulled over in years. Did you have to get out?"

"No. She might have asked me to if she'd smelled alcohol or suspected I was impaired in some way. She asked about medications and whether I'd been on my phone. It was in the console where it always is. Still in there, come to think of it."

"Right! We left in a hurry."

"Yes, ma'am. Best greeting I've ever had." He glanced over his shoulder to where she was busily tearing up lettuce.

She looked up and met his gaze. "I was so glad to see you."

"Same here." The warmth in her eyes filled his chest with sunshine. A few minutes ago he'd pushed her to the point she'd questioned whether they were in this together. What was wrong with him?

"Don't forget the chops."

"Thanks." He rescued them just in time. Another few seconds and they'd begin to char. He was responsible for the stovetop activity and yet she'd had to remind him of it.

Speeding, burning food... what next? He'd better get his act together. He'd never been this distractible. Moving the pans off the burners, he took out a couple of plates and began dishing the food. "How's the salad coming?"

"Almost done. Want some cider with this?"

"Sure. Is the table still set up in the living room?"

"It is, but I didn't light candles or make a fire. I had a feeling we'd head straight for the bedroom and maybe stay a while."

"Good thinking. Let's just eat in here." He brought the plates over to the table, chose the one with the best-looking chop for her and set it in her usual place.

"Just like old times." She set the bowl of salad on the table and put the tongs inside.

"Not a single thing about this arrangement is like old times."

"Yes, it is. We'll sit in the chairs we always take." She gestured to the salad. "Last night you made your own dressing, but if you don't want to take the time, I have a bottle of balsamic vinaigrette in the fridge."

"Let's do that." He pulled out her chair. "I'll get the dressing and the cider."

"Okay." She tightened the sash on her robe before sliding onto the chair.

"Don't cinch it up on my account."

"Habit."

"I know how to break it."

She laughed. "How?"

"Ditch the sash." As he scooted her in, the lapels of her bathrobe shifted, giving him a view of her silky breast. He stepped back and took a deep breath. "Then again, you'd have to spend all your time fending me off."

"You'd get used to seeing me half-naked. It would become old hat."

"Don't bet on it." He took two ciders and the dressing out of the fridge and brought them to the table. "I expected to be less susceptible by now." Twisting off the cap of one bottle, he set it by her place. "If anything, I'm more of a crazed maniac than ever."

"A crazed maniac?" She glanced up at him.

"Yes, ma'am." Leaning down, he dropped a quick kiss on her full mouth before taking his seat. "I want you twenty-four-seven."

"You don't know that yet."

"Yeah, I do. Since I'm getting more obsessed instead of less, twenty-four-seven is a foregone conclusion." He lifted his bottle of cider in her direction. "To the sexiest woman I've ever known."

She tapped her bottle to his. "To the sexiest man I've ever known." She started to take a sip when a phone chimed from the counter. "That's mine."

"Definitely, since mine's in the truck."

"It's Kate's ring. I'd better get it."

"Sure."

She left her chair and the movement loosened her tie. Winking at him, she loosened it a little more before crossing to the counter and picking up her phone. "Hi, Kate. What's up?"

He pointed to his crotch.

Her eyes sparkled as she untied the sash completely and her robe opened a few tantalizing inches. "Everything's just dandy here. Why?"

He began unbuttoning his shirt.

"We know it's open. We just haven't gone back out to close it." Her gaze traveled over his exposed pecs and she licked her lips. "No, that's okay. Thanks, but we'll get it." Propping the phone between her shoulder and her ear, she pulled back the robe to taunt him with a full frontal.

He stood. If she was going to give him an open invitation, he'd take it. But he'd left the bedroom in a huff. As he walked out of the kitchen, she started talking about Nick's favorite cookies and something about CJ eating them, too.

When he came back with the necessary item in his pocket, she glanced at him. "CJ's going to have to start working out."

Jake took the condom from his pocket and walked slowly toward her.

Her eyes widened. "Anyway, thanks for mentioning the truck door."

He unfastened his jeans, released his needy cock and dressed it up for the occasion.

"Yep. Sure. I, um, need to go. Talk to you later." She ended the call and stared at him. "In the *kitchen*?" Her breasts quivered as her breathing sped up.

"Yes, ma'am." He took her phone and laid it out of reach. Circling her waist with both hands, he lifted her to the counter and nudged her thighs apart. "In the kitchen. Gonna tell me no?"

"Are you kidding? I've *always* wanted to do it in the kitchen."

"Then this is your lucky day." *And mine.* Sliding his arms under her thighs, he locked his hands behind her tush and pulled her to the edge of the counter. Perfect height. He slipped right in. All the way. Ahh.

She drew in a breath and gripped his shoulders. "Dinner…"

"Will get cold." He drew back and thrust forward again. Became lost in her green eyes. "Don't care."

"Me, either."

Holding her gaze, he loved her for all he was worth, because she'd always wanted to do it in the kitchen. He could give her that.

25

One more room transformed. Millie would never look at her bedroom in the same way, or the living room. Add the kitchen to the list of places where she'd made love to Jake, and on the counter, no less. He had a talent for creating indelible memories.

After promising he'd do something to salvage their dinner when he came back, he'd gone outside to close the truck door and fetch his phone. She stuck their drinks in the fridge, although drinking warm cider was a small price to pay for another epic orgasm compliments of her resident cowboy.

She picked up the salad bowl, thinking she'd refrigerate that, too, when he came through the front door.

"That truck desperately needs a wash," he said as he walked into the kitchen. "I'm thinking tomorrow."

"I'll help you."

"Ah, thanks anyway. I'll do it."

She smiled. "Don't forget, I'm a cleaning professional."

"And you have to clean all the time. I can't ask you to do even more of it."

"Sure you can. It'd be fun."

He laughed. "I seriously doubt it. Anyway, I brought you this." He handed a bag to her with a flourish. "I've been using yours."

She opened the bag. "Oh, my goodness! This will last me months. Thank you." Glancing up, she tried to read his expression. One bottle of each would have been a nice gesture. Why so many? "You're welcome to use mine, though. You didn't have to replace it, let alone get me all this."

"It's good stuff. I like how it makes my scalp feel. I've never used conditioner, but I might start, since your hair is always so shiny."

"Then you could take some of this back to the bunkhouse when you..." His frown made her pause. They hadn't talked about so many things, and this was another one. The biggest one. "We haven't discussed what happens after Sunday." She put the bag on one of the kitchen chairs. "Maybe we should."

His chest heaved. "Don't see how we can. This is only my second night. Five to go."

"It seems like you've been here longer."

He rested his hands on her shoulders and his gaze searched hers. "Because I've been a pain in the ass?"

"You know you haven't."

"Appreciate that." He took a deep breath. "And I get what you mean about the time span. It feels to me like I've been here longer than twenty-four hours. There's so much to absorb."

"Like what?"

"Living in a house again. Making love to you. It's like I stepped into an alternate reality."

She cupped his face in both hands. "Disorienting?"

"Yeah." He drew her close. "But making love to you steadies me."

"Glad to help."

"That's not the only reason I like it, but it's one of the reasons. When I'm holding you, I know what to do."

She snuggled close and slid her arms around his neck. "Uh-huh."

"That said, we need a timeout to refuel."

"FYI, I'd be fine with eating our dinner cold."

"Well, I wouldn't." He gave her a sweet kiss and let her go. "And I'm going to remedy the situation."

"What can I do?"

"Keep me company."

"Jake, I want to help. You work with CJ. Work with me."

He gazed at her in confusion. "But I want you to relax and let me—"

"CJ enjoys sharing the job with you. I'd enjoy it, too."

"I never thought of it that way." He surveyed the food on the table. "Okay, while I make a sauce, you can cut the meat off the bone, dice it and put it in one of the pans on the stove. Doesn't matter which."

"I'm on it."

Twenty minutes later she sat down to a hot meal of pork and potato hash, salad and the cider she'd returned to the table. "You have skills, cowboy." She dug her fork into the fragrant hash.

He grinned. "Thanks."

She chewed and swallowed. "This is fabulous." She pointed her fork at her plate. "I was starving."

He sighed. "I have yet to figure out how to simultaneously feed a woman and make love to her. I'll work on it."

"Don't get me wrong. You made the right choice, sex first and food second, but the sex made me even hungrier. This tastes like heaven."

"It turned out pretty well." He took another bite and appeared to evaluate as he chewed and swallowed. "Might add some oregano if I make it again."

"You should make it again, on purpose. I'll bet the Brotherhood would love it, too. You should try it on them."

"Maybe I will." He took a sip of his cider. "I heard you say something about CJ eating Nick's sandwich cookies. What's up with that?"

"Evidently CJ and Nick were commiserating about not having girlfriends."

"Because of us?"

"I'm sure that doesn't help, but neither did the wedding. Or seeing Zoe and Seth looking so happy."

Jake nodded. "I can see how that would affect them, but what's the cookie connection?"

"Nick told CJ that the cookies ease the sting of disappointment. Now CJ's hooked on 'em, too." She took another bite of her dinner.

"That's not manly."

She started laughing and almost choked on her food.

"Hey, there." He reached over and rubbed her back. "Take it easy, champ."

She nodded and recovered herself enough to chew and swallow.

"Better?"

"Yes." She wiped her eyes, picked up her cider and took a swallow. "Not manly?" She grinned and shook her head. "Would you rather have them drowning their sorrows in booze?"

His expression was solemn except for the mischief gleaming in his eyes. "That's how it's done. Every cowboy knows that."

"Is that what you do?"

"My goal is to avoid sorrows I have to drown."

* * *

The next morning, Henri invited the staff to the ranch house for a late lunch and a discussion about Friday night's homecoming party for the newlyweds.

The Babes on Buckskins had all chipped in on a gift for Lucy, plus Ed had an additional gift for her. The combination was spectacular enough to warrant an elegant presentation over at Ed's indoor arena. Millie was eager for Matt and Lucy's return and excited about the party, but discussing it highlighted the passing of time and the approach of the weekend, namely Sunday. D-Day.

After a boisterous lunch in Henri's dining room, everyone pitched in to clean up the dishes and then the guys all left. Henri excused herself to handle some email and Kate walked Millie out, clearly wanting conversation.

She paused at the top of the steps. "Garrett seems to be fitting in."

"Uh-huh. Do you think he knows about the Brotherhood yet?"

"He doesn't. The guys are waiting for Matt before they say anything. Jake hasn't mentioned that to you?"

"He hasn't. I'm out of the loop."

"Which is funny, since you're sleeping with the loop master. Or he is until Matt gets back tomorrow night."

"Well, I know nothing." She glanced toward the cottage. Jake's truck hadn't been there when she'd walked over to the ranch house. Now it sat parked in front, the dark blue paint job gleaming. He'd washed it this morning. She looked over at Kate. "Care for a spot of tea?"

"You know it, girlfriend. I've missed our tea breaks." She headed for the steps.

Millie followed her down and walked beside her over the well-worn path between the house and the cottage.

"Jake's truck looks good."

"Yeah, doesn't it, though."

"You have something against clean trucks?"

"No, I just... I'm not sure how to explain."

"We'll get some tea. Tea clears the mind."

"Then I need a couple gallons of the stuff." She walked faster to keep up with Kate. Her roommate never wasted time getting from Point A to Point B.

"Ah. I sense trouble in paradise." Kate reached the steps and was up them and across the porch in no time.

"Not really. I mean, most women would thank their lucky stars for a guy like Jake."

"You'll get no argument from me." Kate went in the house. "I'll make the tea."

"No, *I'll* make the tea."

"Whoa! By all means, make the tea. I didn't know you were so invested."

"Sorry. I'm a little touchy."

"I would say so. Is it okay if I get out the teacups?"

"Please do." She put the water on and measured tea into the pot. "And the honey."

"I'm on it." She set the cups and saucers on a tray along with a jar of honey she took out of the cupboard. "Kitchen or living room?"

"Living room, please." She poured hot water into the pot.

"I'll go move your rocker." Picking up the tray, Kate left.

Millie braced her arms against the counter and took several deep breaths. She'd wanted to help him wash that darned truck. Why couldn't he have agreed to do it together?

Kate had settled down on the sofa by the time she brought the pot in. She added honey to each cup and poured the tea before settling into the rocker.

Kate picked up her tea and blew on it. "I don't know why this should taste any better in porcelain cups than in one of Henri's pottery mugs, but it does."

"I agree." She took a sip. "I need to get back to afternoon tea. With you."

"I would have suggested it, but I didn't want to interfere with whatever was going on over here."

"It's..." Millie sighed and leaned her head back against the carved wood of the rocker. "The sex is great. Better than anything I've ever known."

"Seething with jealousy over her. But do go on."

"But that's the only time I feel as if we're a couple. The only time we have genuine give-and-take. He could have told me what's going on with the Brotherhood. We used to talk about stuff like that."

"If he's a typical male, he doesn't want to waste time discussing extraneous business when he could be playing mattress bingo with you."

"Are you saying sex has ruined our friendship?"

"Not permanently, but you've given him the keys to the candy store. You can't blame the guy for being dazzled by all the goodies."

"Oh, Kate." She grinned. "Nobody breaks it down like you. I'm sure that's part of it. He got pulled over yesterday on the 89 because he was so excited to get back here."

"Jake? Speeding?"

"Yep. But please don't mention it. I think he's embarrassed."

"My lips are sealed, but that's so unlike him. He can be a smartass, but not when he's on the road. Did he get ticketed?"

"No, because he told the officer he was eager to see his girlfriend."

"That's priceless. Then he's crazy about you and the sex is terrific. What's the fly in the ointment?"

"We're living together, but it doesn't feel like it. He washed his truck over at the bunkhouse this morning even though I told him I'd love to help. He takes his laundry there, too. I have to pester him to let me help in the kitchen and he's determined to do the dishes. After he shaves in the morning, he takes his shaving kit out of the bathroom and puts it in his designated dresser drawer."

"You're right. Any woman in America would kill for a guy like that. He stays out of your way except when it's time for sex. Then he's all in. If that doesn't work for you, can I have him?"

Millie groaned. "Call me crazy, but it's not working for me. I don't *want* him to stay out of my way. I want him to be here, really *here,* and not some fabulous cook who's also available for sex."

"Don't broadcast his MO. I'm telling you, you'll get a stampede."

"Are you saying I'm weird because I want more than that?"

Kate smiled. "No, I'm saying you're in love. And so is he, poor slob. I'm guessing he's never felt like this before. Never allowed himself to. He has no idea what to do."

When I'm holding you, I know what to do. "I've tried to tell him, but he—"

"Doesn't hear you?"

"Right."

"Either doesn't hear you or doesn't believe you. Could be either, but it sounds like he's scared."

"Scared? Jake?"

"It would explain why he's not listening. But a big strong guy like Jake would hate admitting that he's afraid."

"He did say living with me is like stepping into an alternate reality."

"One he clearly likes and doesn't want to lose. His strategy is to stick with what he knows you like, the sex and the hot meals, and avoid causing you any trouble whatsoever."

"How do I get through to him?"

"It's tricky. He's spent his adult life avoiding pain. If you tell him he's doing this wrong, he could run."

"I won't say it like that. No blame here. To be fair, we've just started this project. If I thought this trend would change over time, I'd wait it out, but—"

"I doubt it'll change on its own. He's establishing a pattern. One you don't want."

"And if he can't break out of it, we don't have a future."

26

Something was going on with Millie. Jake couldn't put his finger on it, but he sensed a change of mood when they'd made love last night. He didn't know what to do about it.

She'd told him this morning that she wouldn't be home until late afternoon, which wasn't her normal schedule but made sense when she'd described her day. A flood of reservations for this weekend meant prepping more cabins. Bookings always increased when the temperatures rose.

On top of that, she was excited about decorating Matt and Lucy's cabin for their return that night. By tucking all the flowers from the wedding in the dining hall's cold storage, she'd saved most of them from wilting. She planned to fill the cabin with those flowers, turn back the sheets, leave chocolates on the pillows—all the special touches that made her so good at her job.

The cottage had been spotless when he'd arrived Monday night. But this was Thursday afternoon, and he hadn't run the vacuum as he'd planned. The ashes needed to be shoveled out of the fireplace. He'd kept her so busy having sex that she hadn't had time for chores, either.

She deserved to come home to a clean house, and he could make that happen. After locating her supplies, he dived in. Compared to the mess the Brotherhood could make, this was nothing.

By the time she walked through the door a little after five, the house sparkled and the aroma of baking chicken breasts drifted from the kitchen. Damn nice environment, if he did say so.

She took one look around and burst into tears.

"Millie?" He pulled her into an embrace because what else could he do? Were these happy tears? Didn't sound like it.

He held her until she stopped crying. Then he pulled a bandana out of his back pocket and pushed it into her hand. "Here you go."

She sniffed. "Thank you." First she mopped her wet face and then she blew her nose. Created some noise doing it, too. Kind of like an angry goose.

Made him smile. When she was worked up, she forgot about being ladylike. He enjoyed the hell out of that in bed, and here, too, although her tears were confusing. Not what he'd been going for.

She gazed up at him, her eyes still damp. "I'm sorry I lost it. I guess I'm more exhausted than I thought."

"Exactly why I wanted to do this for you."

"And the house is beautiful, Jake. Thank you. And dinner smells delicious."

"Sure didn't intend for you to start crying."

"I'll bet not."

"Why did you?"

She sniffed. "Because you did it by yourself."

"Right, because I wanted to save you the trouble. You've had a busy week and I've been monopolizing a lot of your time."

"But..." She paused as if gathering her thoughts.

Or her courage. Hard to tell which. Either way, sentences that started with *but* were often followed by something he didn't want to hear.

She drew in a shaky breath. "I would like... no, I would *love* us to be a team, like... the Brotherhood."

"The Brotherhood?"

"You know, sharing the load, all for one and one for all."

"That's what I thought I was doing by cleaning the house."

"It was a wonderful gesture." She gazed up at him. "Have you ever cleaned the entire bunkhouse as a surprise for your brothers?"

"Of course not. That would be weird."

"Because you're all on equal footing. That's what I'm looking for. Equal footing."

"I don't know what you're talking about. There's no comparison between the Brotherhood and us." Frustration crowded his chest and he couldn't tamp it down. "Guys get it all out, they mix it up, but when it's two people, a man and a woman, it's... different."

"Why?"

"It just is. It's like a damned minefield."

"I don't see it that way." She wiggled out of his arms. "I realize you were subjected to that as a child, but you and I aren't living in the middle of a minefield."

"Are you sure?"

"Yes, absolutely. I—"

"I cleaned the house and fixed a chicken dinner because I thought you'd be pleased, and—"

"I am! But—"

"You are not! You're in tears because I did it by myself while you were working your tail off. If that's not a minefield, what is?"

"You're giving me what you think I want, but you're not—"

"What could be better than coming home to a clean house and a hot meal?"

"Letting me help you wash your truck! Setting up laundry day where we do it together! Letting me into your life the way you've let your brothers in!"

A thick, heavy blanket of soggy despair settled on his shoulders. She was yelling. He was yelling. "I'm sorry, Millie. What you're asking... I don't know how..." He swallowed. "I don't know how to do that."

"Of course you do. You do it every day in the bunkhouse."

"This is not the bunkhouse, damn it!" Yelling again. Keys. Where? Oh, yeah. In the dresser drawer, where they wouldn't encroach on her space.

He walked back to her bedroom, pocketed the keys and headed for the front door.

"What, you're leaving?"

"I don't have a better idea."

"I do! You could stay and we could work this out."

"'I don't know how to do that, either."

"You do it all the time with your brothers!"

"You are not one of my brothers." And he couldn't treat her like she was. She was so much more. And clearly he couldn't handle more.

Getting out to the truck was a chore with lead weights hanging off every part of him. He couldn't seem to start the engine, either. Had to hurry, in case she came after him. He didn't want that.

Oh, yeah, he did. Two days ago, she'd rushed out and climbed on the running board to get to him. Likely wouldn't be doing that tonight.

The engine roared to life. He backed out, not sure where he was going. He ended up in front of the bunkhouse. As he grabbed his hat off the dash and climbed down, the scent of sloppy joes drifted in his direction. CJ had taken one of his suggestions.

Maybe Garrett had put the meal together. The new hire made going inside tougher. Garrett wasn't one of them. Not yet.

Squaring his shoulders and taking a deep breath, he opened the screen and the front door. Rafe and Nick looked up from the checkers game they were playing beside the wood stove. They exchanged a glance and stood.

Rafe kept his voice low. "I need to fetch wood for the stove. Want to help?"

Jake nodded. Garrett and CJ were laughing about something in the kitchen. Probably hadn't heard him come in.

"I'll go, too." Nick grabbed his jacket and hat from the back of his chair. "Can always use more wood."

Leo came out of the bathroom and paused. "What the—"

"We're fetching wood." Rafe put on his hat. "Going out the front."

"I'll help." Leo unhooked his hat and jacket from pegs in the wall above his bed.

Ridiculous as the subterfuge was, Jake appreciated the effort. The woodpile was out back. The kitchen door was the logical access point. But this trip had nothing to do with wood.

He headed in that direction, anyway. The moon was up, so he could see where he was going and watch for skunks. They loved the shelter of that woodpile.

No critters with a white stripe showed up as he approached. He turned around to face his brothers. "It's over."

Their muttered responses showed off an impressive vocabulary. The Brotherhood had a talent for swearing when the occasion called for it.

Nick blew out a breath. "Looks like I'll be needing more cookies."

"Thanks for the thought, but I don't need—"

"Don't knock 'em 'till you've tried 'em, Jake. CJ's a big fan."

"Enough about the cookies." Leo stepped closer and rested a hand on Jake's shoulder. "What happened, bro?"

"I cleaned the house to surprise her when she came home. She didn't like that."

"*Whaaat?*" Leo stared at him as if he'd lost his mind.

And he might, any second, now. "She didn't object to me cleaning it. She thanked me and said it looked nice. She objected because I did it by myself."

"And you broke something," Rafe said. "Some glass doodad she treasured."

"I didn't break anything. Used all her products. Figured she'd prefer that. The place looked great."

Leo squeezed his shoulder and stepped back. "Then I got nothin'. Maybe an alien's taken over Millie's body like we saw in that movie one time."

"Or she was hungry," Nick said. "That makes me cranky."

"I had dinner in the oven."

"Then nothing makes sense." Nick's forehead wrinkled in confusion. "Don't women love it when we vacuum and stuff?"

"Generally they do," Leo said. "Maybe you should have timed it so she could watch you muscle that bad boy around the house."

"Who knows? She wasn't happy about me cleaning when she wasn't there, that's for sure. And the other day she accused me of being the Lone Ranger."

Rafe peered at him. "Why?"

Damn. He hadn't meant for that to get out. "I, um, got pulled over coming home on the 89. Wouldn't let her share the blame."

Rafe's eyes widened. "Why'd you get pulled over?"

"Speeding."

They gasped in unison.

"No big deal."

Nick's mouth was still open. "How fast?"

"About twenty over."

Rafe studied him. "This is more serious than I thought. You're in love with that woman."

"No, I'm not. I just—"

"Rafe's right, bro." Nick eyed him intently. "That must have been the day you went to Great Falls for the hay nets and the cookies. Am I right?"

"Yes, but—"

"I remember thinking you were falling for her. We were shooting the breeze about this and that. Then I mentioned Millie and your whole expression changed."

"It's not love." Jake tugged his hat lower. "It's just... you know... sex."

"It's way more than that," Leo said. "You've had girlfriends before. This is different. I think we've all seen it, but with Garrett around, we don't talk like we used to."

"And we still can't," Rafe said. "Which is why we're out here freezing our asses by the woodpile. It's a family matter."

Jake met Rafe's gaze. "I know, which makes this tough."

"Let me ask you this. Do you *want* it to be over?"

He sighed. "It isn't going to work, Rafe. She wants us to function as a team." He gestured toward them. "Like the Brotherhood does."

He nudged back his hat. "There's a major problem with that concept. Millie's—"

"A woman." Jake grimaced. "I've noticed."

"Me, too," Nick said. "I mean, not *noticed* like I was checking her out. I wouldn't do that, but women, Millie included, are different from us."

Leo rolled his eyes. "Thank you, Captain Obvious."

"For your information, Leo, I'm not talking about physical differences, although there are plenty of those. I'm saying their behavior is different, too. Personally, I like that about 'em."

"I do, too," Jake said. "Or I did, until tonight."

Rafe shoved his hands in his pockets and rocked back on his heels. "I've learned this about women—you think they're mad at you for one thing and it turns out to be something else entirely. Did you screw up without realizing it?"

"Hey, Rafe." Nick looked at him. "How's he supposed to know if he screwed up if he didn't realize it?"

"Occasionally, Nicholas, some of us can remember the screw-up upon further contemplation. Maybe if Jake recollects his actions over the past three days, he'll have an *aha* moment."

"Except he won't go *aha*," Leo said. "That's when you have a brilliant idea. When you remember a screw-up, it's an *oh, crap* moment."

"We're veering off the subject." Rafe turned to Jake. "What about it? Anything coming to you?"

"Nope."

"Then let's revisit the previous question. Do you want to end it?"

"No, damn it! But I don't know what to do!"

Rafe's attention swung to Nick and Leo. "Now that Matt's coming home, we need to call a meeting of the Brotherhood tomorrow and brainstorm this problem. Without Garrett."

"I'll arrange that," Nick said. "I'll ask him to get more chicken breasts at the market so we can have them again Saturday night. Those were good eats." He turned to Jake. "No offense."

"None taken."

"I'll ask Henri to give him another errand in town," Leo said. "Can I tell her why?"

Rafe nodded. "She'll be on board. By morning she'll know about this, anyway. Jake, you okay with us butting into your personal business?"

His chest swelled with gratitude as he gazed at his brothers. "Yeah. I need all the help I can get. But this talk has built up a powerful thirst. I could use an ice-cold brew. Or three."

"Sounds good to me," Leo said.

"Me, too." Rafe started back around the house. "I'll have to stick with one, though. I'm picking up Matt and Lucy tonight."

"Want me to ride along? I'll lay off the booze if you need company."

Rafe shot him a grin. "Nah. I don't think you should be dealing with two blissed-out honeymooners tonight. Drink as much as you need."

"Cookies work great, too," Nick said. "Unfortunately, CJ and I ate all the ones you brought."

"No worries." Jake clapped him on the shoulder. "I prefer to drown my sorrows in booze."

27

Millie had read plenty of books in which the broken-hearted heroine couldn't bring herself to touch a bite once the blow had fallen. She suspected those ladies had consumed a large meal before the heartbreaking incident, which would explain their lack of appetite.

She, on the other hand, hadn't eaten much of anything since breakfast. She devoured two large chicken breasts and most of the salad Jake had left in the fridge. He'd probably planned on serving a veggie, too, but she wasn't up to cooking. Just eating.

And drinking. She had one hard cider with dinner and followed it up with another one in front of the fire. Jake had arranged logs on the grate and stuffed a bunch of crumpled newspaper underneath. The fire roared to life with a single match. That cowboy knew his way around a fireplace.

And a kitchen. And a bedroom. Now there was a depressing prospect. She was more than happy to eat the food he'd fixed, but climbing into the bed they'd shared would be a way bigger challenge.

She wasn't up to it tonight. She'd be on the couch, instead. Sure, he'd made love to her there, but only once.

Her fancy king bed, though... it had been the scene of countless... ah, better not go down that bunny trail. Her dream bed might be forever compromised. Which sucked.

So many things sucked regarding the present state of affairs. At the top of the list? She'd have to see him almost every damned day from now until one of them croaked.

Until death do you part. Ha, ha. They wouldn't be married to each other, but they were both hitched to the Buckskin. Had she fully appreciated that fact before starting this program? No, not really.

Naïve and optimistic, that was her. She'd been so convinced they could make a go of it given a chance. This week had been that chance.

Even now, their spectacular crash and burn wasn't real to her. The shock of it didn't register until she forced herself to go into the bedroom for the quilt and a pillow. He'd turned down the sheets and left a piece of chocolate on her pillow.

Gasping and fighting tears, she ran out of there like her hair was on fire. No. *No, damn it.* This couldn't be happening. It was a bad dream. She'd wake up any minute, now.

She took a blanket and pillow from Kate's bed, got another cider, and built up the fire.

Sleeping in her clothes would be extremely uncomfortable, but she wasn't going back in that room to get a nightgown. Not tonight.

Halfway through the cider, drowsiness overtook her. She was such a lightweight. And so damned tired. No wonder, considering the wedding, the revelation about Jake's marriage fears, and the resulting experiment in cohabitation that had morphed into a royal fustercluck.

Leaving the bottle on the coffee table, she checked the fire. Almost out. If only the burning sensation in her chest would be that cooperative. She replaced the screen and returned to the couch.

Stripping down to her bra and panties, she snuggled under the blanket and burrowed into the pillow. She reached for the switch on the table lamp beside the couch and clicked off the light. Moments later, she turned it back on. Darkness was not her friend.

But sleep might be. She didn't have to set an alarm. All her hard work today meant she had less to do in the morning. She could sleep in. Whoopee.

* * *

The click of a key in the lock jerked her awake. She sat up and rubbed her eyes. Why was there light outside the window? And why was Jake standing in the doorway looking like death warmed over?

His gravelly voice matched his unshaven chin and bleary eyes. "I thought you'd be gone."

"What time is it?" She didn't sound all that great, either.

"Nine-thirty."

"In the morning?"

"Yes, ma'am." He took off his hat and ran his hands through his unruly hair. "You're usually out of here by nine."

"Not today."

"I see that." He put his hat on again and his gaze flicked over her.

Oh, yeah. She was wearing her undies. She pulled the blanket up and tucked it under her armpits. "You look like hell, Jake."

"Can't imagine why." His grin flashed, his teeth white against his bristle, almost a typical Jake smile. Except there was no light in his eyes. "I feel terrific."

"I'm glad for you."

"Why are you on the couch?"

"What are you doing in my house?"

"Came by to get my stuff." He rubbed his chin. "Realized it was all still here when I couldn't find my shaving kit."

"Oh. Right." Her grand plan to make his exit complicated had failed. He'd simply left everything and walked right out the door. She gestured toward the hall. "Have at it."

"Why aren't you at work?"

"None of your beeswax."

He gazed at her a moment longer. Then he broke eye contact. "I won't take long." His boot heels clacked noisily on the hardwood floor as his long strides took him down the hall and into her bedroom.

The sound was unfamiliar, out of place. But why? Ah. Most of the time he'd been barefoot. Ready for anything. Her chest tightened.

Hangers banged against each other in the closet. Her dresser drawer squawked in protest as he jerked it open. Maybe he was reacting to the turned-down sheets and chocolate the way she had.

The heavy-duty zipper on his duffle rasped and he reappeared, his breathing uneven as he walked into the living room. Earlier his expression had been carefully blank. Not anymore.

She looked away from the pain in his eyes. Self-inflicted, but that didn't make it any easier to witness.

"I, um, didn't expect to find you here."

"Clearly."

"But since I did, this might be our only chance to talk."

Her heart thumped faster. "About what?"

"This isn't exactly a private breakup."

She met his gaze. His mask was back on. "Nope."

"We'll be seeing each other tonight over at Ed's. For the party."

"The party is the least of our concerns. We'll be seeing each other every day for *years.*"

"Yes, ma'am." He swallowed. "Guess we'll get used to it eventually, but tonight—"

"I'll do my level best to act normal. Lucy and Matt deserve that. Everyone does, come to think of it."

"You're right. I'll do the same."

"I can't speak for you, but I refuse to let this ruin my life at the Buckskin." Brave words, and she intended to live up to them, one day at a time.

"That goes for me, too. What I meant is that by tonight, the word will be out."

"Have you mentioned it to anyone?"

"I drove over to the bunkhouse last night."

A rush of relief caught her by surprise. He'd left in such a terrible mood that he could easily have spent the night parked in some remote area nursing his wounds. "I'm sure being with your brothers helped."

"Yes, ma'am."

"Did you drown your sorrows?"

"I gave it a shot." He gestured to the cider bottle on the coffee table. "How about you?"

"I'm a washout at that. Evidently I'm not manly at all."

His mask slipped just enough to allow a soft smile. "Wouldn't want you to be."

Her breath caught. "Jake..."

The smile disappeared. "Better go." He touched two fingers to the brim of his hat. "See you later, Millie."

She clenched her hands and tightened her jaw. She would not call out. She would not go after him. She would *not*.

But damn, she wanted to. If she ever got her hands on that cowboy again, she'd shake him until his teeth rattled. What an idiot.

She was no better, though. She'd ignored the danger signs and barreled ahead, allowing herself to fall in love with a man who was capable of recklessly throwing away happiness with both hands.

_28_

Jake glanced around the bunkhouse kitchen table and the tension that had plagued him since seeing Millie this morning eased. Like old times, sitting around and making jokes with the Brotherhood.

In the middle of the afternoon, each of them had coffee mugs in their hands instead of bottles of hard cider. Rafe had begged a couple dozen chocolate chip cookies from the dining hall and those were going fast.

Not having Seth there had bothered Jake a few months ago. Not as much these days. Seth was happier than he'd ever seen him. Change happened. Everyone adjusted. Matt had taken the leadership role and now that he was back from his honeymoon he could fully claim it.

As promised, Nick had sent Garrett off to buy chicken for Saturday's dinner. Henri had come through with a sizeable list to keep their new hire busy in town for a couple of hours.

Matt was regaling them with his pathetic attempts to surf in Waikiki. Evidently Lucy had proved to be better at it. "Bested by my bride." He laughed. "But hey, my legs are tan for the first time in my life."

Jake gave him a nudge. "Gonna drop trou and show us?"

"No, I am not. I only take off my Wranglers for one person these days."

"Yeah, yeah," Nick said. "Rub it in, bridegroom."

"Sorry. Didn't mean to. Not when we have a wounded warrior in the group. Which brings us to you." Matt turned in his chair, his expression serious. "What the hell is going on, Jake?"

"I don't know."

"She expects them to be a team," Rafe said. "She wants their relationship to follow the Brotherhood model."

"Huh." Matt looked thoughtful, then shook his head. "She just thinks she does."

"Thank you." Jake let out a breath. "I tried to tell her that, but—"

"Hey, it's a natural conclusion for her to make. She sees how you are with us and she wants that."

"I'll bet she doesn't want belching contests," Nick said, "not to mention pee—"

"Yeah, let's *not* mention that," Matt said. "Women are becoming part of the mix. We need to keep our embarrassing traditions to ourselves."

Nick frowned. "What do you mean by *becoming part of the mix.* Are we referring to Lucy? Or Kate and Millie, too?"

"All three of them. But Kate and Millie know us a little better. Lucy still has a somewhat... idealized image of the Brotherhood."

"So do Kate and Millie," Rafe said, "if you want to get right down to it. We've never had chugging contests when they were around or written our names in the snow afterward. We need to keep it that way."

"Yep." Matt poured himself more coffee and passed the carafe to Leo when he signaled with his mug. "Bottom line, we need to break it down and figure out what about the Brotherhood experience Millie really wants." He glanced at Jake. "So you can supply it."

"What if I can't? What if the kindest thing I could do is leave her the hell alone?"

"You've been living with her for three days." Matt held Jake's gaze. "Are you ready to give up?"

Jake heaved a sigh. "No. When I saw her this morning, I... it was rough. On both of us. The way things are, I don't know if we can even be friends anymore. At the very least, I'd like to repair our friendship, for her sake."

"Then let's go with that. What's her biggest complaint?"

"She called me the Lone Ranger. I shoulder all the responsibility. The cooking, the dishes, the laundry, washing my truck. She wants to help, but I... don't see the need."

"But she does. Why not let her help out if that's what she wants?"

"Because he's trying to be nice," Rafe said. "What's wrong with treating a woman like a queen? He cleaned the entire house and she was upset. Go figure."

"Jake, you can do my laundry any time." CJ grinned at him. "I promise I won't be upset."

"Bite me, CJ."

"I see what Matt's getting at," Leo said. "Let her help you wash the truck. She'd probably be good at it since cleaning is her strong suit. If doing laundry together is important to her, then why not?"

"I'll tell you why not." Jake's gut churned. "We won't agree on how to do stuff. And we'll argue."

"So what?" Leo swept a hand around the table. "We argue. No big deal."

"I can't argue with Millie."

"Why not?"

"I don't trust myself."

Matt stared at him. "If you're saying you'd get physical, I don't believe that for a minute."

"I'd never lay a hand on her, but I could start yelling."

"That's not the end of the world," Matt said. "People yell sometimes."

"My parents yell all the time." Jake had nearly recovered from this morning's hangover but his headache came back with a vengeance. "Once they get going—"

"Is that how you see yourself behaving with Millie? Because I've never seen it around here with us."

"That's different."

"Why?"

"Because we're all guys. It's different when it's a man and a woman. It can quickly get out of hand. It's better if I do things myself."

Rafe leaned forward. "But Millie's the other half of the equation. We've all worked with her for years. She doesn't go looking for an argument."

"Excellent point," Matt said. "Neither do you, Jake. Will you and Millie disagree if you share a daily routine? You bet. But you're not your father and I doubt Millie's anything like your mother."

"She's not, but..." He took a deep breath. "It's what I grew up with. It's what I know. The odds that I'll repeat the pattern are—"

"Hang on." CJ put down his coffee. "I just thought of something. Your folks—do they have any friends?"

"Not long-term ones. They're not exactly a fun couple to be with. But what does that have to do with anything?"

CJ smiled. "Millie called you the Lone Ranger, but you're not alone, not even close. You have the Brotherhood. And a creed to live by."

Jake swallowed. *What would Charley do.* Charley wouldn't have stomped out of Millie's house, that's for sure. "I violated our creed. I hurt Millie."

"Yeah, you did." CJ nodded. "But none of us are saints. Bottom line, you're not going to repeat your dad's pattern. Not on our watch."

"Hallelujah!" Matt threw his hands in the air. "CJ, you're a genius."

"Glad you finally realized it."

Jake blinked. "You'll monitor my behavior?"

"Damn straight," CJ said. "Not that we even need to, but since you're scared to death you'll go off the rails, think of the Brotherhood standing on either side of the tracks to make sure you don't."

"And if that's not enough," Matt said, "you'll have the Babes keeping an eye on you, too, plus Kate and Lucy."

The knot in Jake's chest slowly loosened. "That…" His throat clogged with emotion. "That's… you're right. The Brotherhood would never let me get away with being a bastard. Or the Babes, either."

Rafe laughed. "Or Kate and Lucy. They're mighty."

"But what now? After the way I left, I can't just hit rewind and expect her to fall into my arms. Millie and I aren't on the best of terms."

"I can vouch for that," Rafe said. "Kate's talked to her and she's ticked."

"Besides." Matt pushed aside his coffee mug. "Running back over there today looks wishy-washy, like you can't make up your mind about the relationship. This is too important to risk giving her that impression."

"That's for sure," Leo said. "I'm thinking it's grand gesture time."

Excitement churned in his gut. "It is." *What would Charley do?* And then it hit him. Talk about obvious. "But not tonight because we have the party at Ed's. I'd like to make my move tomorrow night."

"Don't see why not. Nothing's scheduled." Matt gazed at him. "Seems like you have this grand gesture in mind already."

"I do." Jake glanced around the table. "And since I'm not the effing Lone Ranger, I need the Brotherhood to help me pull it off."

29

At four on the dot, Millie got Jake's text. *Been doing some heavy-duty thinking. Not quite ready to talk about it yet, but would greatly appreciate it if you and Kate would ride to the party with Rafe and me. If it's not too weird for you.*

She walked to the doorway of Kate's room, where she was putting things back in her closet. "Jake just texted to ask if we'd ride to the party with him and Rafe."

Kate looked over her shoulder. "Rafe said that text would be coming. You don't have to do it, though. I'll ride over with you like we planned."

"What do you think he's up to?"

"God knows." She went back to hanging up clothes. "Rafe said they had a meeting of the Brotherhood this afternoon but he couldn't tell me what it was about. Right. Like I can't guess they were talking about the situation between you and Jake."

"Must have had some effect on him. He says he's doing some heavy-duty thinking."

Kate took a jacket off a hanger and closed her closet door. "Think he wants to come back?"

"Kinda sounds that way, doesn't it? Mentioning that he's been thinking and would like us to ride together like we usually do."

Kate put on her jacket. "Like I said, you don't have to."

"No, but... oh, who am I kidding? I'm nuts about that cowboy. I want to wring his neck, but it's not like I never want to see him again. Let's go with them to the party."

"Okay." She started for the door. "I'll text Rafe when I'm closing up the kitchen. I should be back here somewhere around seven."

"Thank you. You've been great and, just so you know, Jake's not moving back in here."

Kate paused by the door. "Hey, if you decide to take him back, it's fine with me if he lives here. I just hope you don't cave without some groveling on his part. And assurances he won't bolt again."

"Ha. He'll have to jump through flaming hoops of fire before I'll agree to give him another shot. And I'm serious about him not moving back in. We tried that. It didn't work."

"Poor guy didn't know a good thing when he had it. Gotta boogie. See you at seven." She hurried out the door.

Retrieving her phone, Millie typed. *OK* and sent it to Jake.

His reply was instantaneous. *Great. See you then.*

She stared at his text. Anticipation, yearning, excitement—familiar emotions connected with Jake. Today she added a new one—caution. Jake had the power to lift her higher than she'd even been... and thrust her into the deepest well of misery.

He wouldn't get away with that again.

* * *

Riding shotgun in Jake's truck with Kate and Rafe in the back seat was surreal, as if she'd time-traveled to a moment before Jake had moved into the cottage, before they'd become lovers.

In place of his former morose and silent mood, Jake clearly wanted to make conversation "Any ideas on the surprise for Lucy?"

"My guess is a saddle," Rafe said. "She's been taking barrel racing lessons from Ed and Matt says she's found her sport. She loves it. But she's never had her own saddle."

"That would explain why barrel racing is a part of this welcome home party," Kate said. "I'm impressed that Lucy's willing to show off what she's learned tonight. She has to be jetlagged."

"I spoke to her for a few minutes when I was making my rounds this morning," Millie said. "She's the one who suggested making her first public ride after the honeymoon. She figures jetlag will keep her from getting nervous. She's expecting they'll present her with a Babes on Buckskins T-shirt."

"She might get one tonight," Rafe said, "but that's not the surprise. It's something more significant, but the Babes like to play things close to the vest."

"Like the Brotherhood?" Kate nudged Millie's seat with her knee.

"I don't know what you're talking about." Jake glanced at Kate in the rearview mirror. "We're an open book."

"Except when you're not."

"Okay, maybe we keep a few select things private."

"Yeah," Rafe said. "Like full-moon skinny-dipping in Crooked Creek."

Millie made a face. "The Brotherhood is welcome to that stupid ritual."

"Why?" Jake flashed her a grin. "What's wrong with it?"

"That creek's fed with snowmelt." She shivered. "I stuck my toe in it once in July. Still freezing."

"That's the point." He kept his attention on the road. "Gets your blood pumping."

"I can think of better ways to accomplish that."

He sucked in a breath. "Yeah, me, too." He flipped on the turn signal and slowed as they approached the entrance to Ed's impressive layout.

Rafe gazed out the window. "Every time I come out here, I'm amazed. I know she won a lot of competitions, but I doubt many barrel racers end up with a spread like this."

"Henri says she's also a financial genius." Jake guided the truck down the paved road and past the imposing stone and wood ranch house.

"Guess Teague will be helping out tonight." He sounded cheerful about the prospect.

Aha. The other shoe dropped. He'd wanted to arrive with her so Teague wouldn't start getting ideas. "Guess so." She peeked over at him. "It'll be nice to see him again."

"Sure will. Great guy." He was smiling.

She almost laughed. His protective instincts were wasted. After she'd spent three nights with him, Teague didn't have a chance.

He parked in front of the arena as trucks pulling horse trailers drew up on either side of them. Each of the Babes trailered her horse over to Ed's for these events and the Brotherhood handled the bulk of the unloading.

Rafe helped Kate out before heading off to the trailer nearest them. Normally, Jake should have done the same, but instead he put his hand on Millie's arm before she could unfasten her seatbelt. "I just need a few seconds."

She glanced at him. "To confess that you wanted me to ride with you as a signal to Teague? I figured that out."

"That's not the only reason." His fingers tightened briefly. Then he moved his hand. "I wanted a chance to say something."

Heat sluiced through her. A few words from Jake could turn her world upside down. Again. She had to be careful. "Look, I don't know what your intentions are, but—"

Unfastening his seatbelt, he turned toward her. Floodlights on the eaves of the arena provided plenty of illumination inside the cab. "I don't want to lose our friendship." His gaze was intent, his forehead creased with worry. "Getting it back might be impossible, but I hope not. I'd hate to think we'll be at odds for…"

"Weeks? Months? Years?"

"One day has nearly killed me. If I had to go weeks, months, or God forbid, years, without your smile, I couldn't take it."

Her throat tightened. "But last night you—"

"I was a jerk. Asking you for anything now is pushing it. But I'll ask anyway. Regardless of what happens between us, can we please do whatever it takes to keep our friendship?"

Her thumping heart was loud in the silence. "Whatever it takes? What does that mean, exactly?"

"I'll tell you what it means for me." He started to reach for her but drew his hand back. "Sorry. I keep forgetting I can't touch you any old time I want. I gave up that privilege last night."

Her resolve took a hit. She quickly repaired the damage. "Yes, you did." She would *not* feel sorry for him.

He nodded. "And I may not get it back, but I'll never treat you like that again. When I stomped off, I violated our friendship, which means the world to me. I just hope I haven't wrecked it for good."

She gripped her seat belt strap and fought the urge to absolve him of everything, to cradle his face and smooth away the lines of distress. She didn't want him to suffer. But she didn't want to suffer, either.

Dragging in a shaky breath, she unfastened her seat belt. "We'll see how it goes."

"That leaves me some hope. Thank you. I'm needed for the unloading, but will you wait and let me help you out?"

"I'd rather not." She opened her door, climbed down and started toward the arena.

Kate stood by the open double door, waiting. "Well? Did he grovel?"

"Yes, and I hate seeing him so miserable. I almost—"

"But you didn't." Kate took her by the shoulders and gave her a supportive squeeze. "You listened and got out of there."

"How do you know?"

"I watched you guys. It was like a silent movie, but I got the gist."

"You watched?" She turned around and looked at Jake's truck. "Wow, it's like looking in a department store window."

"Yep. He had on his earnest face and you were looking adorably resolute. I crossed my fingers that it wouldn't end in a lip-lock and it didn't. Props to you, girlfriend. What was his pitch?"

"He admits he was a jerk and promised he wouldn't repeat what he did last night. He wants to preserve the friendship."

Kate smiled. "Nice opening gambit. Classy. You do realize he's after more than friendship, right?"

"Yes. But unless he's ready to give up his previous attitude, he won't get it. And I've heard nothing that makes me think he's changed his MO."

"Attagirl." She turned and glanced into the arena. "We'd better get in there. They're almost ready."

Millie followed Kate into the arena, an indoor facility Ed had constructed years ago for practicing her barrel racing skills. At eighty-five, her time around the barrels still beat all the other Babes, plus most riders who participated in the sport worldwide.

A set of bleachers sat at one end facing the start line for the circuit. Millie glanced at the spectators. "Peggy and Pam's husbands are here. I can't remember the last time they both made it to one of these."

"Must be why everything was set up so fast. They were here to help unload Dust Devil and Latte."

"I want to ask Ron about his last speaking tour. Peggy said he was booked into some big venues."

"Let's sit with them. That would be a good strategy."

"For what?"

"Backing Jake off so he doesn't try to monopolize you."

Millie laughed. "What are you, my manager?"

"Yes, I am. I thought I could trust him with your heart, but now I'm not so sure."

"Kate, I adore you."

"Backatcha, sweetie. Let's go chat with Ron and Lee."

Millie climbed the bleachers and Kate engineered the seating so Millie sat between Ron and her. No room for Jake to horn in. Good. That lowered her stress level.

Ron and Lee were both sixty-something, like their wives. Ron, a silver-haired smooth talker with a degree in psychology, had built a career as a motivational speaker and traveled a lot. Lee, a sturdy man with a luxurious mustache, was nearing retirement as Apple Grove's fire chief. The phrase *salt of the earth* described him exactly.

Two very different personalities, but the Babes on Buckskins had brought them together and they were fast friends. Millie embraced the rare opportunity to find out what was going on with them.

When Jake and Rafe took seats behind her and Kate, a shiver down her spine told her Jake was within arms' reach. But she kept her focus on Ron, who'd had a series of adventures on his latest speaking tour.

Then Ed announced Lucy's barrel-racing debut. She'd be on Muffin, the horse she'd used during her lessons and the veteran Ed had ridden in competition for at least twenty years.

Millie stood and cheered with everyone else, although the Brotherhood, who'd all ended up sitting behind her, drowned out the rest of them. Matt was the loudest of all. Sweet.

Lucy thanked Ed and blew a kiss to Matt. Then she was off, flying around those barrels. Muffin likely could have done the course on his own, but Lucy stayed with him and turned in a credible time.

Amid more cheers and applause, Ed presented Lucy with a Babes on Buckskins T-shirt. Grinning like a little kid, Lucy put it on over her shirt. Then Teague came out with a hand-tooled saddle, which Ed announced was a gift from the Babes. Lucy was clearly stunned.

"Called it," Rafe muttered from his seat behind Kate.

"Bet Jared Logan made that baby," Jake said.

"Yep." Matt's voice was husky. "Ed asked me to oversee the process, although all the Babes had input. Lucy seems to like it."

"Probably does," Nick said. "Since she's tearing up."

Ed picked up her mic. "One more thing before we switch to the regular competition. Lucy, you and Muffin make a good team. He's yours."

Lucy started blubbering and protesting.

"This isn't a random impulse." Ed wrapped an arm around Lucy's shoulders and spoke into the mic. "I've shocked the bride, but the Babes and I've talked about this for several weeks."

Lucy grabbed the mic and sniffed. "Thank you, but I can't take Muffin."

"Yes, you can and you should. I need a new challenge, so I'm training Suede, a rambunctious four-year-old with promise. It's with great joy that I pass Muffin on to you, Lucy. He has at least ten good years left in him and he knows the ropes."

Chaos reigned for another few minutes, but eventually Lucy agreed, with many hugs involved, to accept the gift of Muffin.

Millie looked at Kate. "I did not see that coming."

"I didn't, either, but it makes sense. Ed on Muffin was an unbeatable combination. A challenge keeps life interesting. It's good to have to work for what you want." She turned around. "Right, Jake?"

"Right, Kate." He sounded amused.

Millie was especially fond of that tone, when his voice held an undercurrent of laughter. That was the Jake she'd fallen in love with. But he was far more complicated than that. After all the years of contact with Jake, did she know him at all?

30

Evidently Kate had appointed herself Millie's protector, and Jake didn't begrudge her that. Served him right. Kate had moved over to Henri's place to give him private time with Millie. He'd blown that golden opportunity, which was his own damn fault.

But it meant he wouldn't get much access to Millie during the barrel racing event or the party Ed threw at her spacious home afterward. His only consolation was that Teague didn't get access, either. That was partly Kate's doing and mostly Millie's. She dodged Teague the whole evening. Did his heart good.

But he had Millie in the passenger seat on the way home. Well done, him. She looked both happy and sleepy. If only he hadn't ruined everything, he'd be able to take her back to that big bed and make love to her. Instead, he had to drop her off at the cottage with Kate.

Rafe climbed into the seat Millie had recently vacated. Typical Rafe, he chose not to wear a seatbelt rather than change the specs to fit a frame twice as big as Millie's. "All things considered, that went well."

"Sure did for Lucy."

"Wasn't too bad for you, either, hotshot. It's clear Millie doesn't hate you."

"That still leaves a lot of room for improvement. She wouldn't let me help her out of the truck when we got to the arena. She specifically refused."

"Do you blame her?"

"No. I blame myself, which makes it hurt twice as much. Things are worse than before we had sex. I used to be allowed to hug her, dance with her, grab her around the waist when we were kidding with each other. Now it's strictly hands-off."

"Buck up. We have a plan, right?"

"After tonight, I wonder if it's doomed."

"Is that any way to talk? You were fired up this afternoon and we're all on board. I did some reconnaissance during the party and I have some options for you to consider."

"Like what?"

"Henri wanted to know if you had a plan and so I told her what it was."

"You did? But what if she tells—"

"Come on. Henri's never betrayed a confidence in her entire life. She asked if she could tell the Babes, and I said she could."

"Damn it, Rafe, the more people who know, the more likely Millie will hear about it."

"Let me ask you this. Did the Babes keep that saddle deal a surprise for weeks?"

"Yeah."

"I think they can keep this under wraps for less than twenty-four hours. And I'm glad I said something, because Ed and I have come up with an awesome idea. I also—"

"Wait. *Ed* is part of the process, now? What the hell, Rafe?"

"Hear me out. This could be great. I was talking with Kate, and—"

"You told Millie's best friend? Are you insane?"

"Relax, bro. I didn't describe the plan, I just wanted to get a sense of how Millie felt about you. She said something that gave me an idea."

"I'm afraid to ask."

"Look, you're the one who came up with the bold move. Don't chicken out, now."

Jake sighed. "Lay it on me."

"Millie told Kate you'd have to jump through flaming hoops to get her back."

"That sounds like Millie."

"Remember that white horse of Ed's, Silver? The one who's trained to—"

"Holy crap. You want me to jump that horse through flaming hoops."

"I do! It's a crazy stunt, but—"

"But it's perfect." He grinned. "It's what Charley would do."

"I know, right? He was a master of the grand gesture. Like the time they had a fight and he hired a skywriter. Epic."

"I thought of doing that, but Millie remembers it, too. It would be like I couldn't come up with my own ideas." He pulled into his usual parking space beside the bunkhouse. "To be fair, I didn't come up with the flaming hoops." He glanced at Rafe. "I owe you one."

"You don't owe me a damn thing. We're in this together."

"Thanks, bro." He lifted his fist and Rafe tapped it with his. "Can't wait to tell the guys about this."

"Yeah, they'll love it."

"Does Ed still have everything we need? It's been years since she performed that stunt for us. Millie wasn't even here yet."

"Which makes it all the better. Ed's kept it since she still has some film crews from California using her property. The hoops are a handy prop. A crew used it, and Silver, a few months ago. Works fine."

"Excellent. I've never jumped through a flaming hoop, though. I should probably—"

"Ed suggested you come out for a few run-throughs in the arena." He hesitated. "One slight catch. Teague's the expert on the hoops. He'd supervise your run-throughs and would be the one who sets up everything and breaks it down."

Jake nodded. "Figured. That's fine. He's the one who gave me the kick in the butt I needed to go after Millie. I'm grateful. If he's willing to help, I'll pay him whatever he wants to charge."

"My guess is he won't take it."

"Probably not." He smiled. "In his shoes, I wouldn't, either. He's a good guy."

"Just not good enough for Millie."

"Damn straight."

***

Late the next afternoon, Jake left Ed's place with a new respect for Teague. He clearly loved working with horses, especially Silver, and he proved to be an expert in handling the flaming hoops. He explained every safety precaution he'd take to guarantee that nothing other than the hoops would catch fire.

He was also the most gracious loser Jake had ever met. At the end of the run-throughs, he shook Jake's hand and wished him and Millie a long and happy relationship. Did it with a smile, too.

Jake's schedule for the next few hours was packed and that was a good thing. Kept him from obsessing about the night's outcome.

Because Garrett was cooking his popular chicken dinner, Jake had evening barn duty. He'd have a short time to shower and change clothes before dinner.

Garrett had slipped into the cooking job during Jake's nights at the cottage and the Brotherhood seemed okay with it. Chuck wagon stew night had been replaced this week by the party over at Ed's and nobody had commented on that, either.

No telling how things would shake out after tonight. It all depended on Millie. But he couldn't focus on her or he'd go nuts.

He was a little late for feeding, so he drove straight to the barn. Nick had brought the horses in from the pasture and was delivering hay flakes.

Jake grabbed a pair of gloves from the tack room and started down the barn aisle to fetch a wheelbarrow from the back. "Sorry I'm late."

"No worries. Did it go okay?"

"It went great. It's fun jumping a horse through a flaming hoop. Teague knows his stuff, too. We don't have to worry about burning down the pasture tonight."

"That's a relief."

"Hey, you left the new wheelbarrow for me. You didn't have to—"

"You need all the good juju you can get. It was the least I could do. Did Henri fix you up with a mask?"

"She took a black strip of material and cut eyeholes in it. She thinks I need the tight lace-up shirt and pants, but I'm not into spandex." He loaded hay flakes into the wheelbarrow.

"Yeah, I'd skip that, too. You have the white hat."

"And a grey shirt that I bought a size too small by mistake. Oh, and Henri insisted I had to tie this red strip of cloth around my neck." He started delivering hay. "I don't know what it's supposed to do for you. It's not a bandana. She showed me a picture and damned if he didn't always wear it."

"This is gonna be one hell of a night, bro."

"No kidding. I'm glad we're finally letting Garrett know about the existence of the Brotherhood."

"Kind of necessary under the circumstances. Hey, I told you a few days ago that we wouldn't let him take your spot in the kitchen, and yet—"

"It's the way things have worked out this week. That's okay. I mean, if Millie... well, I don't want to speculate about Millie. But no matter what, I'm making chuck wagon stew next Friday night."

"That's what I wanted to hear. We've gotta keep that going. It's my all-time favorite meal."

Jake paused. "All-time favorite?"

"Absolutely. It's amazing, and because it's your special recipe, our bunkhouse kitchen is the only place in the world I can get it. I value that."

Jake's chest tightened. "Thanks, bro." The phone in his pocket chimed. Pulling it out, he checked the screen. "It's Matt. Dinner's almost ready."

"Then let's pick up the pace."

After the horses were fed, Jake gave Nick a lift back to the bunkhouse. Showering and shaving meant he was late to dinner, but that couldn't be helped.

When he walked into the kitchen and took his place at the table, Matt stopped talking and turned to him. "I just finished telling Garrett the plan."

"Okay, good." Jake took the platters of food as they were passed to him and filled his plate. If he was lucky, he'd need the fuel. "But I assume you didn't mention—"

"Nope. Waiting for you."

"I'm glad he filled me in," Garrett said. "That explains the tight shirt and the red scarf."

CJ grinned. "Jaunty accessory, bro."

"I'm sure Henri could fix you up with one, CJ." Jake tucked the trailing ends under his collar to get them out of the way while he started eating.

"I'd forgotten about that scarf." Rafe looked amused. "Never questioned it when I watched those old shows, but wearing something bright red around your neck isn't too smart when the bad guys are gunning for you. Makes you an easy target."

"Nobody outguns the Lone Ranger," Nick said. "He can wear whatever he wants."

Garrett laughed. "Yes, he can. You look good, Jake."

He chewed and swallowed. "Thanks." He glanced at Matt. "Anytime you're ready."

Matt nodded and looked across the table at Garrett. "There's something special about this group and we've chosen tonight to tell you about it."

"Oh?" Garrett put down his fork.

"Providing you with this information is the reason we gave Millie and Kate for why I'm here and Lucy's having dinner at Henri's."

Garrett's focus sharpened. "Go on."

"All of us at this table were hired at different times and for different reasons, but we have one thing in common. Henri and Charley took us in when we had nowhere else to go. We owe them..." He paused and shook his head. "More than I could begin to describe."

"I see." Garrett took a deep breath. "That explains a lot."

"When Charley died four years ago, we lost a man we'd come to think of as our father. As we flailed around, searching for something to hold onto, some way to comfort Henri, we turned to each other. The Buckskin Brotherhood was born."

"Wow. A band of brothers. I sensed...something...but I didn't—"

"We're a tight bunch, as you can imagine. We'd do anything for each other. Including crazy stunts like tonight's deal."

"It's out there, all right."

"And it's not even the wildest thing we've ever done. There's a lot more to tell, even more you'll have to just experience. But since you agreed to go along tonight, you need to know about the Brotherhood. The subject will come up." Matt paused. "Over the next few months you'll learn more about us. And we'll learn more about you."

"I get it." Garrett glanced around the table, his expression solemn. "Thanks for including me."

31

As often happened, Kate had brought home leftovers from the dining hall to share with Millie. They'd just finished eating when Millie's phone chimed.

She left the table and picked it up from the counter. "It's Henri. She and Lucy just finished dinner and looked outside. Evidently there's a spectacular sunset and moonrise combo developing. They're driving over to the pasture to get a better look and invited us to go along. Henri's taking the apple tarts she baked this afternoon."

"Yum. I love those things. I'm game."

"Me, too. That's one of the few disadvantages of this cute cottage. It sits in a low spot and you don't get a good sunset view."

Moments later she climbed the gentle slope up to the house with Kate already three steps ahead. That woman could not walk slowly to save her soul.

Henri already had the truck running. Millie got in the back seat with Kate and buckled her seatbelt.

"We're off." Henri put the truck in reverse. "Charley and I used to do this all the time. The view from the pasture is so much more open than the one from the porch. After all, we live in Big Sky Country. We need to pay attention."

"I wonder if the guys have even noticed, considering they were going have this discussion with Garrett about the Brotherhood," Millie said. "I hope it's going well." For someone who'd pleaded with her last night to keep their friendship alive, Jake had been strangely silent today. Not even a brief text.

"I'm sure everything went fine." Lucy turned toward the back seat. "Like I told Matt, Garrett just needs to know about the Brotherhood. He won't expect to be invited into it. Not yet, for sure, and maybe not ever. They all have to wait and see."

"I wasn't sure what they were going to do," Henri said. "But since they formed the Brotherhood, it was their call what to tell him and when."

"I can relate to being the new person in a tight group." Kate glanced at Millie. "You and Henri were lifesavers. The guys took a little longer to warm up, but now it's like I've been here forever. Garrett will get there eventually, too."

Lucy nodded. "It takes a while. When we flew in from our honeymoon, it was the first time I fully realized this was my home, now. Which reminds me." She pulled out her phone. "I spent some time today culling the Hawaii pics so I'm finally ready to show them off. I took tons, but so many were repetitive."

"I'd love to see them." Millie leaned forward.

"Here you go." Lucy scrolled to a shot of Matt standing in the surf. "Start with this one." She handed her phone back. "That's our first trip down on the beach. But wait until you get to the ones of Matt surfing. They're hysterical."

Millie took the phone and held it so Kate could see. "You two look so happy."

"We were. We are." Lucy pointed to the screen. "That's at the luau. Matt tasting poi. Ever had it?"

Kate laughed. "Once at a friend's house who'd been there and had some shipped home. I'm not a fan."

"We weren't, either. There's me doing the limbo. There's Matt, falling on the sand while trying to do the limbo."

Millie grinned. "I think Matt needs to stick to being a cowboy."

"That's what he said. Next are the surfing pictures. We—"

"Lucy." Henri pulled the truck to a stop. "We're here."

"Right. We'll finish them later."

"Sure." Millie handed back the phone. "Great pictures, Lucy. You guys..." She trailed off. Henri had parked in the middle of the pasture. About twenty yards ahead of them was a giant hoop, with a second about ten yards behind it.

Both were shooting flames. "What the heck is *that*?"

"Just get out," Henri said. "Everything will make sense in a minute."

"You know what this is about?"

"I do."

"Lucy? Do you know?"

"Yes. You should probably stand in front of the truck."

Millie looked over at Kate. "Do you know, too?"

"I don't, but I'm starting to get it. Millie... *flaming hoops.*"

"So what? I—" *He'd have to jump through flaming hoops.* "How could Jake know—"

"I told Rafe last night that you said that."

Clapping her hand to her mouth, she scrambled out of the truck and hurried around to the front bumper.

From across the meadow, seven riders galloped toward her, the horses' hooves making the ground shake. The cowboy in the middle rode a white horse. A red scarf around his neck fluttered in the wind. He wore a tight gray shirt, snug jeans, a white hat... and a black mask.

He drew closer to the first hoop and the three riders on either side split off, veering around the flames. The white horse gathered himself and leaped through the fiery circle, raced forward and sailed through the second one.

Oh, Jake. An adrenaline rush left her trembling.

About ten feet away, he pulled back on the reins and came forward slowly. His gallant steed pranced, arched his sleek neck and blew through his nostrils.

She gulped. "You jumped through flaming hoops."

"Yes, ma'am." He swung down from the horse and dropped the reins to the ground. "It was your requirement." As he approached, he untied the mask and handed it to her. "This is for you. My days of being the Lone Ranger are over."

Dazzled by the intensity in his blue eyes, she clutched the material and struggled to breathe. "Just like that?"

"Just like that."

"But people don't change overnight."

"They can if it's important enough." He took a deep breath. "I love you, Millie Jones."

She gasped.

Sweeping off his hat, he dropped to one knee. "Will you marry me?"

"*Marry* you?"

"Yes. I don't have a ring. I wasn't going to rush that, but you have my love and my word that we'll have that happily-ever-after. We—"

"You've really caught me by surprise."

"You don't want to?"

"Of course I want to, but—could you stand up, please?"

He rose to his feet and took a quick breath. "I've loved you from the first day I laid eyes on you but I'd never been in love before, so I didn't know what was wrong with me. Or right with me. Rafe told me I was in love with you and I didn't believe him, but he was right. We don't have to get married right away. We can have a long engagement so you can make sure I'm—"

"Jake, could you please be quiet for a minute?"

"Yes, ma'am."

She took his hat, dropped the black cloth into it and handed both to Kate. Grasping his hands in hers, she lifted her face to his. "I've loved you ever since I laid eyes on you, too. I've been waiting and hoping for this moment ever since that day. If you want a long engagement, I guess we can have one, but I don't see the point. I believe in you and your brothers believe in you or they wouldn't be here lending their support. We can't go wrong."

"That's a yes?"

"That's a hell, yes." Releasing his hands, she pulled his head down and kissed him.

With a groan, Jake wrapped her in his arms and kissed her back, which set the Brotherhood to whooping and hollering.

Lifting his head, Jake gazed into her eyes and smiled. "They're happy."

"Not half as happy as I am."

"Or me." He went back to kissing her.

Sooner or later they'd have to stop, since they were standing in the middle of the pasture with a bunch of folks looking on. But maybe if they kept kissing, everyone would just leave them there.

Then Jake would carry her off on his white horse, just like in a fairytale. And she would get her happily-ever-after. Because Jake had promised.

* * * * *

Cowboy CJ Andrews faces the challenge of a lifetime in BABY-DADDY COWBOY, book three in the Buckskin Brotherhood series!

CJ loved every second of his brief affair with beautiful and witty Isabel Ricchetti. Under different circumstances, she could have been the one. Too bad her coffee shop's in Seattle, not Apple Grove, Montana.

But when an unplanned pregnancy turns their carefree fling into a serious commitment, CJ's priorities shift. Isabel may be looking for a long-distance co-parenting plan, not a relationship, but CJ can't imagine being a long-distance dad.

He also can't imagine keeping his distance from his baby's mommy.

* * * * *

New York Times bestselling author Vicki Lewis
Thompson's love affair with cowboys started with
the Lone Ranger, continued through Maverick, and
took a turn south of the border with Zorro. She
views cowboys as the Western version of knights in
shining armor, rugged men who value honor,
honesty and hard work. Fortunately for her, she
lives in the Arizona desert, where broad-shouldered,
lean-hipped cowboys abound. Blessed with such an
abundance of inspiration, she only hopes that she
can do them justice.

For more information about this prolific author,
visit her website and sign up for her newsletter. She
loves connecting with readers.

VickiLewisThompson.com